SCp

sparks

ALLY KENNEN comes from a proud lineage of bare-knuckle boxers, country vicars and French aristocracy. Prior to becoming a writer, she has worked as an archaeologist, a giant teddy bear and a professional singer and songwriter.

Her first novel, BEAST, published in 2006, was shortlisted for the Booktrust Teenage Prize and the Carnegie Medal, and won the 2007 Manchester Book Award. Her second novel, BERSERK, won the North-East Teenage Book Award and the Leicester Book of the Year Award 2008.

Ally lives in Somerset with her husband, three small children, four chickens, and a curmudgeonly cat.

No woman has ever beaten Ally in an arm wrestle.

Also by Ally Kennen

BEAST
BERSERK
BEDLAM

sparks

Ally Kennen

MARION LLOYD BOOKS

First published in the UK in 2010 by Marion Lloyd Books
An imprint of Scholastic Children's Books
Euston House, 24 Eversholt Street
London, NW1 1DB, UK
A division of Scholastic Ltd.
Registered office: Westfield Road, Southam, Warwickshire, CV47 0RA
SCHOLASTIC and associated logos are trademarks and/or registered
trademarks of Scholastic Inc.

ISBN 978 1407 11108 7

A CIP catalogue record for this book is available
from the British Library.

Printed and bound in Great Britain by
CPI Bookmarque, Croydon.
Papers used by Scholastic Children's Books are made from
wood grown in sustainable forests.

1 3 5 7 9 10 8 6 4 2

www.scholastic.co.uk/zone

For Wilfred, my bright spark.

CONTENTS

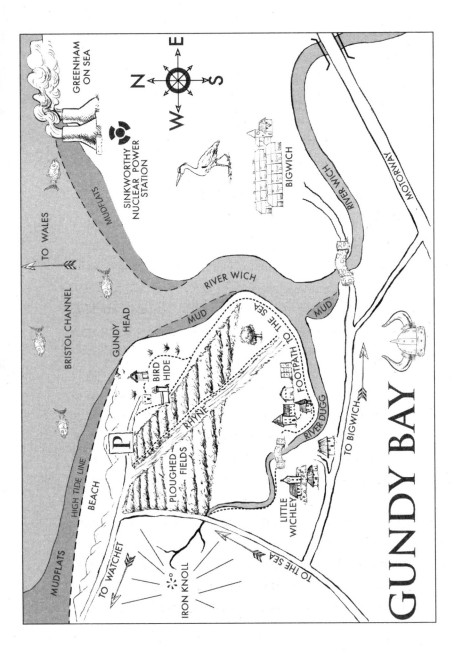

GUNDY BAY

Grandpa

Rain dribbled down Carla's neck as she slipped and skidded over the muddy river path. A few feet below, the River Dugg gushed and foamed, smelling sourly of mushrooms and oil. Half a mile downstream the Dugg ran into the Wich estuary, which then flowed out to sea. Grandpa said the source of the river was a spring up on Iron Knoll. He said if you drank a cup of the water, you got special powers for twenty-four hours.

It was on Carla's list of Things to Do.

She shoved aside the metal sheeting and entered Grandpa's garden. Pushing through dripping nettles, she raced up to the barn. "Grandpa," she called, "I've got something important to tell you." She knew something was wrong as soon as she stepped inside. Grandpa's barn was usually full of noise. Drills whirred, saws roared and grinding machines buzzed as Grandpa worked. He was building a small boat and it was nearly

1

finished. But today Carla heard only the rush of the river from the end of the garden and the rain drumming on the skylight.

Freya, the children's mother, said the barn was like an exploded rats' nest. There were crates of screws, nuts and bolts, and vast coils of wire were stacked against the walls. Grandpa had lengths of pipe and metal propped in the corners, and his stuff covered every surface: silver foil and pogo sticks nestled in amongst chainsaw chains, cans of spray paint and old paperback novels. A line of crystals hung in the dirty window, so when the sun shone the place was filled with rainbows. Napoleon, a large stuffed black bear, towered in one corner. He and Grandpa had been together since Grandpa's navy days. Legend had it that the bear had once saved Grandpa from drowning. Napoleon had a singed back and a missing foot where Grandma had chucked him on the bonfire before Grandpa had managed to rescue him. But the centre of the barn was dominated by *Valkyrie,* Grandpa's boat. Grandpa had been spending days and nights on her. She was a small, flat-bottomed sailing boat and was awaiting a final coat of paint. Other than that, she was finished. Or as finished as she could be, Grandpa said. He wouldn't know what needed doing until he took her out on the water – which might be this weekend. Carla hoped she'd be one of the very first crew. Grandpa had high hopes that *Valkyrie* would win the Gundy Bay boat-building competition.

Grandpa was Good with His Hands. He could mend anything, from backfiring cars to snowstorming televisions. He sorted out sputtering tractors, blunt lawnmowers and silent generators. And in return for a hot dinner delivered at seven o'clock every night, he fixed things for the members of Little Wichley Ladies' Baking Club.

But where was he?

Yesterday, after school, all three children had gone over to Grandpa's barn – he had a little cottage at the front of the garden, but he only went in there to sleep, and not always then, as he had an old, dusty couch behind a mountain of used car tyres in the barn.

He'd looked up from a paint chart as the children had trooped in. "You're only here for cake! Why don't you get your mother to make one, instead of thieving from me?"

"She only bakes cakes when she feels inspired," said Penny. She took the paint chart and examined the colour he had circled.

Duck-egg Blue.

"If I only did things when I felt inspired, I'd never do anything," huffed Grandpa, removing the lid from a battered flowery tin to reveal half a thickly iced chocolate cake. He fished in his overalls for his penknife, wiped the blade on his trousers and cut four large slices.

"You haven't washed your hands," said Penny,

eyeing his oil-grained fingers. At nine, she was particular about such things.

"I'll eat yours then," said Grandpa, giving her a piece anyway.

"Who made it?" asked Carla. "Not Mrs Davies?"

"No, this is Mrs Roper's, thank God," muttered Grandpa. He turned to Woody, who at twelve was only eleven months younger than Carla. His birthday was at the end of March and Carla's was at the beginning of May. Every April, they were the same age. The problem, as far as Woody was concerned, was that as he was two inches shorter than his sister, everyone assumed he was much younger.

"You're quiet," said Grandpa, giving Woody the biggest slice of cake. "What's up?"

"He's being bullied," said Penny.

"Am not," said Woody, giving her a murderous look.

"He is," said Penny. "He wet the bed when he stayed over at Gary Bradley's. Now the whole school knows and Mikey Dobbs's gang are harassing him."

"I spilled my water," protested Woody. "I never wet the bed."

"Lots of sailors do wet the bed," said Grandpa, ruffling Woody's hair. "It's to do with being surrounded by all that water. The water in their bodies wants to get out and join the ocean. When I was at sea, there was a steady drip, drip on to the deck, and rivers of pee pouring out the portholes. And that's a fact. That's why sailors sleep in hammocks – so they don't have to wash out sheets."

Penny stared at Grandpa. "Are you telling the truth?" she asked.

Grandpa stared back, deadpan. "Are you calling me a liar?"

"Yes, because—" began Penny.

"Have my chocolate cake," said Carla, pushing it into her sister's mouth. "I'm full."

Grandpa winked at Woody. "Your blood is full of sea salt," he told him. "Just like mine."

"I still didn't wet the bed," grunted Woody.

Now Carla, wiping the rain from her face, looked round for her grandpa. She noticed a puddle of blue paint pooling over the floor from under *Valkyrie's* trailer. Grandpa was always in his barn, *always*. Unless of course he was out fixing something for the Baking Club, but that was unlikely as his dinner was due to arrive at the garage door in five minutes and Grandpa never missed that. Maybe he was having a nap – something he'd been doing a lot recently. Carla crossed the barn and peeked behind the vast pile of tyres at the back wall.

"Grandpa," she whispered. Because he was here after all, lying on his couch with his head tucked into his chest and his knees drawn up, like a little boy sleeping. But he was too still, and too quiet. And he looked so *small*. When Carla stepped over and touched his arm, he felt cold. "Oh," said Carla. A white button hung by a single thread from his cuff. "Grandpa," babbled Carla, "we're getting a puppy. Mum finally said yes. Woody found an advert in the paper and tomorrow we're going to look. It's half-term, you see, no school. . ." Carla straightened Grandpa's collar. "There are two boys and a girl. They're a spaniel cross." She stopped talking and a tear fell from her eye and landed with a plop on Grandpa's shoulder, blotching his shirt.

Grandpa wasn't breathing.

There was a rushing in her head, like the river was flowing from one ear to the other, as she crumpled to the ground.

Someone was calling.

"Magnus? Magnus? Time to down tools, old man. Where are you? I nearly drowned bringing this over." Carla sat up and watched as a short, plump woman with damp grey hair appeared with a steaming dish of food.

"Miss Hame," whispered Carla – she couldn't speak any louder – "Miss Hame, I think . . . I think my grandpa has died."

"I doubt it," said Miss Hame. "I've made his favourite, spiced lamb stew. He wouldn't miss that." Through blurry eyes, Carla watched as Miss Hame shoved aside an oil can with her elbow and set down the stew.

"He'll be having forty winks," she said, stepping closer and patting the rain from her coat. "Do get up, dear – this floor is *so* dirty."

Carla shut her eyes.

There was a pause.

"Oh," gasped Miss Hame. "Oh, *Magnus*!"

Opening her palm, Carla found a small white button.

"Grandpa?"

Napoleon's Neck

Woody was eating with the pig. In the last twenty-four hours Mum had developed a very short temper and when Woody had dribbled gravy down his front for the third time, she'd yelled at him.

"If you are going to eat like a pig, then go and eat with it."

Carla found her brother sitting on the garden wall, gloomily throwing potatoes for Aurora, Mr Jones-next-door's sow.

"It's not my fault I spill everything," said Woody. Grandpa had said that Woody was clumsy because he had the brains of a tall man.

"You're going to be at least six feet tall, only your arms and legs haven't caught up yet," Grandpa said. *"Your brain sends out tall-man messages to the rest of you. So things are a bit uncoordinated when your hands can't reach what you THINK they can. Don't*

worry," Grandpa continued. *"Everything grows at an uneven rate. If I plant a packet of seeds, they don't flower at exactly the same time. It's nature."*

"Mum says you can come in now," said Carla. "But I've brought out your pudding in case you don't want to. It's only tinned peaches." Woody took the dish of peaches from Carla and emptied it over the wall. They watched as Aurora demolished them.

"Everything's rubbish," said Woody. He had red eyes from crying. Carla looked away. Everyone kept bursting into tears. She'd found Mum in floods over the oven, and Dad had been sniffing over breakfast. Even Penny, who tended to keep her head about most things, had shut herself in her room and would only come out for meals. But Carla, apart from the one tear she'd shed when she'd found Grandpa, hadn't cried at all.

"Have a good cry," Miss Hame had advised, rather bossily. "It helps, you know." But Carla didn't want to cry. It was impossible that Grandpa wasn't here any more. She couldn't believe it, even though she'd seen him with her own eyes. And anyway, she knew where he was – at the funeral parlour of his old mate Mr Salt, the undertaker. Mr Salt said the children could visit any time they wanted, as the funeral wasn't scheduled until next Saturday. There was a whole week to get through, and Carla didn't even have school to distract her as it was half-term. Mum had cancelled going to see the puppy. Carla understood why, of course, but she wished Mum had rescheduled the visit for a better day. Then she felt mean about her wish. Grandpa had just died, and here she was moping over a puppy. But she couldn't help feeling disappointed. She'd wanted a dog for *years*. They only had a one-eyed cat called Nelson, who had no time for anyone but Dad.

"Only last week Grandpa told me he didn't know how he was going to stick being buried next to Grandma," blurted out Woody, kicking the wall with his heels. "He said she'd drive him bonkers. He said he'd have to rise from the grave and find another, more peaceful one. And he wasn't joking."

Grandma had died years ago, when the children were small. But Carla really didn't want to think about her right now. Woody slid from the wall and plodded listlessly back to the house, leaving his dishes in the grass. Carla found her feet taking her to the bottom of the garden. Before she knew it, she was walking along the riverbank. The water rippled and sparkled in the sunshine. In two minutes Carla was in Grandpa's garden. Surely if she went through the nettles and into the barn, she'd find Grandpa, hammering and whistling? He'd see her and start singing.

"The sweetest girl I ever saw
Sat sucking cider through a straw. . ."

Everything was how he'd left it. Napoleon the bear grimaced down at her, *Valkyrie* sat on her trailer and a mug half full of black coffee sat clouding on Grandpa's workbench. Carla crept behind the tyres to the couch. She hoped that if she wished hard enough, he'd be there. But of course he wasn't; there was only a dent in the faded blue cloth where he had lain. Carla took Grandpa's spanner from the bench and cuddled it close. She found herself lying on the couch, curled up, just like Grandpa had been. She thought this might be the moment when she cried, but she didn't. The couch smelled of oil and dust and mud and Grandpa's washing powder.

"Grandpa?" whispered Carla.

She watched the hand of Grandpa's big station clock tick round the dial. After Grandpa had left the navy he'd worked at Bigwich Station for twenty years, and when he'd retired they'd given him the clock that had hung above the platform before they'd replaced it with a digital one. She couldn't believe it was only yesterday that she'd found him. Everything had moved so fast. After the doctor had been (Carla thought that was odd – why call a doctor for someone who had already died?), Mr Salt the undertaker had whisked Grandpa away.

And now Carla was alone. She saw the cake tin up on its high shelf. Without really knowing why, she padded over and stretched up to reach it. There were a couple of slices of cake left, a bit stale-looking but edible. Carla was about to replace the lid when she noticed something. An envelope was taped to the underside of the lid. And it had her name on it.

For Carla Moon. To open after I've gone.

Carla frowned. How could he have known she would go for this tin? Carefully she opened the envelope and unfolded the letter inside.

My dear, lovely Carla,

I thought you'd find this letter, and I was right. You've always had an extraordinary affinity with chocolate cake. Anyway, I've been feeling odd and ill these few weeks and have an inkling I'm on my last legs. Carla, don't be sad. I've had a wonderful life and I'd rather pop off now than be a dribbling wreck later. I'm not going to be all maudlin, but I will say you and Woody and Penny have lighted up my life. By the time you find this letter I expect I'll be in the churchyard, cuddled up to Grandma (!)

But I have a request. An old sailor like me is never really at home unless he is on the sea. I always fancied a Viking funeral, where my remains were sent out to sea on a burning boat at sunset, to sail off into eternity. I even made some enquiries, but it turns out it's illegal, so sadly I've had to forget that dream.

But Carla, could you do something for me? Napoleon has a small box concealed under the fur at the back of his neck. (He's hollow, did you know that?) It's got some letters inside. They're only silly old things, written years ago. Could you make a raft and set fire to the letters and send them off down the

*river at high tide? I'd rather you said goodbye to me
there than in the churchyard.*

*Love to you, Carla, my beautiful granddaughter,
Your Grandpa.*

Carla read the letter again and then her gaze fell upon
Napoleon. Directly she was feeling along the back of
his neck. His fur was stiff and slightly damp and
smelled of mothballs. She lifted up a flap around his
scruff and immediately found what she was looking for:
a small, flattish box, tied with red wool.

Grandpa's letters.

She eyed the box. She didn't want to read them yet.
They were Grandpa's private letters. He might not like
it. She could put them in a wooden fruit crate, or make
a simple raft from some of Grandpa's wood. It would
be easy to carry out Grandpa's wish. Very easy.

Carla replaced the letters and stroked Napoleon's
fur. He could look after them for a bit longer until she
worked out what she was going to do with them. But
just suppose, she wondered, just suppose she tried to
give Grandpa the funeral he *really* wanted. Could it be
done? Was there any way a thirteen-year-old girl could
give her grandpa a Viking funeral? She'd have to be
quick; the official funeral was next Saturday, only six
days away. And according to Grandpa's letter, the
whole thing would be illegal, which meant no grown-
ups. And there would be some challenges involved in
getting Grandpa from the funeral parlour on to the ship.

And the ship itself, of course – where would she get one of those? And how would she get it to go out to sea? No, it couldn't be done. It was much too difficult, and dangerous.

She looked at *Valkyrie*, sitting proudly on her trailer.

"How do you know she'll float?" Penny had asked Grandpa.

"Because of the planning in her construction," he said. *"As well as the high-grade wood, the precision carpentry, the finely balanced knees—"*

"Spare me," interrupted Penny. "You don't know she won't sink."

"Yes, I do," said Grandpa. *"Sometimes you know you can do amazing things."*

"Yes," muttered Carla. "And maybe I can do this amazing thing." She thought of Woody and Penny.

"But not on my own."

Penny and Woody

"**P**ush the door any further and you bust Harold's skull," shouted Penny. Harold was their hamster. Carla didn't like him very much – he was smelly and once he had bitten her thumb and drawn blood – but even so she didn't want to be responsible for his death. She hammered on Penny's door. "We have to talk. Let me in."

"Keep the noise down," howled Mum from downstairs. "I'm on the telephone."

"Oh for goodness' sake," muttered Carla, slumping to the ground.

Woody watched her from the top step. "It can't be that important," he sighed.

Carla puffed out her cheeks. This wasn't going to be easy. She spied the small sailing boat on the alcove above the stairs. It was a model of the first boat Grandpa had ever built: *Julie*.

"The ground is too still for me," Grandpa had said. *"I prefer being on the water."*

"OK," she said. She beckoned Woody over. "Penny, I'm going to tell you something. You don't have to come out, though that would be nice. This is a secret, OK? Don't tell anyone, especially Mum." Woody picked at the hem of his trousers. He didn't seem interested. Carla wondered if she was mad. In order to do this, they were going to work impossibly hard. They would have to tell whopping lies, break the law in a thousand places and learn about all kinds of stuff in a very short time. She didn't even know if it was possible. She needed a team of superheroes, or at least a sailor, a tractor, a boat and a great deal of paraffin. All she had was one small miserable brother who was starving himself to death and an even smaller sister who wouldn't come out of her room. She listened to her mother murmuring downstairs.

Of course we want flowers. Dad loved flowers. . .

Carla lowered her voice. "This is about Grandpa," she said. "It might be the most important thing we do in our lives." Woody looked up. His face was blotched and he had a crust of dried snot stuck to his cheek. He didn't look like a superhero at all. Carla told herself not to worry.

Anything was possible.

"How do you know you can't do something?" Grandpa had said. *"Until you've tried to do it?"*

"I found this." Carla passed her letter to Woody.

16

"But why is it to you?" Woody's eyes welled with tears as he read it. "Did he like you better than me?" Carla cursed herself. But she had to show them, otherwise they wouldn't understand.

"He says you lighted up his life," said Carla. "That's pretty good."

Woody sniffed. A hand shot out of Penny's door. "Give."

Woody passed the letter over and the hand shot back in again. "I never knew Napoleon was hollow," said Woody, brightening. "And we could easily set fire to Grandpa's letters for him. I'd like that."

It wasn't going to work, Carla told herself. Penny and Woody were too little and too sad to go through with it. She hated seeing them like this. Perhaps she should just let the grown-ups take charge of Grandpa after all. Penny's door opened. Clad in purple pyjamas and holding the letter, she advanced towards Carla. She eyed up her sister.

"I think Carla is planning to burn more than letters," she said. "Correct?"

Carla swallowed. "Maybe," she said.

"You'd better come in," said Penny, pushing her door wide open. Woody looked puzzled but followed Carla. The children settled on Penny's bed. Penny always kept her room tidy without ever having to be nagged. Carla wished she could be like this. She loved things being tidy, and everything in its place, but never seemed to manage it. She had to remember to put things away and

17

make her bed and not drop her clothes on the floor. Whereas Penny just did these things naturally. Carla considered her bedroom tidy if there was a path of clear carpet from her bed to the door. Woody never seemed to hang on to his stuff for very long. He'd lose his toys, and his books were always getting ripped or found, swollen to monstrous proportions, in the garden. His bedroom always seemed empty. Carla looked at Penny. Her little sister, always pale, was now so white Carla could see the veins through her skin. She looked like a ghost. Naturally Carla didn't tell Penny this, but she worried about it all the same. Woody wasn't eating and Penny wasn't moving much. She was stagnant, and Mum and Dad were too busy and sad to notice.

"It can't be done," said Penny, hugging her pyjamaed knees. "It's too difficult, and you'd need a grown-up, and what about a boat? And what if he came back to shore?" She glared at Carla. "I don't want Grandpa being messed around with. We'd make a pig's ear of it and end up going to prison. And what will Mum say?"

Carla thought for a minute or two. Naturally she'd worried about all these things, and many more.

"I'm lost," said Woody. "Anyone want to tell me what you are talking about?"

"It can be done," said Carla slowly. "Anything is possible, remember? And we DO have a boat. We have Grandpa's boat: *Valkyrie*. And of course we have to work out about the tides and things. But you know what he says about the Bristol Channel."

"*The fastest, most treacherous strait in the world, where a spring tide will outrun a grown man. Forget Cape Horn; beware of Gundy Bay and the mudflats of Little Wichley!*"

"I think once we've launched him and the tide race has got him, it'll be fine," said Carla. "As long as we catch a high tide, set the sails and tie the tiller."

"You don't know that," said Penny.

"No," said Carla. She felt exasperated. "Look, I don't know if we can pull this off. But we can try. Look at the letter. Look."

Carla took Grandpa's letter and read out loud.

"'*An old sailor like me is never really at home unless he is on the sea.*'

"So how can we have him buried in the churchyard after he says something like that?" Carla glared at the others. "Next to Grandma!"

"You have a point," said Penny thoughtfully. "I never met her but I've heard the stories. Imagine spending eternity next to Grandma."

"Hey!" burst out Woody. "I think I know what you two are on about."

"At last," sighed Penny wearily.

"But I can't quite believe it," he said. "You don't really want us to, to . . . to—"

"Yes," said Penny, butting in. "She wants us to give Grandpa his very own Viking funeral."

Valkyrie

Grandpa said *Valkyrie* was his dream boat. He'd been building it, on and off, for two years, and it was finally nearly complete. *Valkyrie* was a simple boat, similar to the flatner type people used in bygone times to row over the area's shallow inland creeks and rivers and sail in the bay for all sorts of jobs.

"But not Viking funerals," said Penny.

"*Valkyrie*'s perfect," said Carla, ignoring her. "She's made for getting out over the mud without running aground. She's light, beautiful and most importantly – " she paused – "Grandpa made her."

"He may prefer that she isn't burnt after all his work," said Penny. "Surely he'd have liked us to have her?"

"We've already got *Julie*," said Carla firmly. "Woody is the only one who goes out boating with Dad these days." Woody had been quiet throughout the conversation. He kept rereading the letter and going to the door to check no one was listening. Carla could tell, despite her comments, that Penny was interested in the plan, but as for Woody, she had no idea.

"What do you say, Penny?" asked Carla. "Shall we just, say, look at our options? Do a bit of research?"

"Count me in," said Penny. "I must be insane. But Grandpa deserves it."

Carla breathed out. She'd thought Penny was going to be the tricky one. "You know there are some major problems," she admitted. "The funeral is in six days, and Grandpa is already at Mr Salt's. We'll have to bust him out."

Penny grimaced.

"It's going to be really hard, and I'm not saying that we're going to succeed, but we could just look into it, couldn't we?"

"We'll do more than that," said Woody, breaking in. "We're going to do it. Grandpa deserves it."

The first job on Sunday morning was to inspect Grandpa's boat. Mum was blowing her nose when the children trooped through the kitchen.

"Woody Moon," she said, pointing, "eat something."

"Later," said Woody. "We're going out for some extremely fresh air." He winked at the others. Mum thought fresh air was the best thing in the world.

"But. . ." The phone rang, cutting her off. "Don't go anywhere until I get rid of whoever this is," she hissed as she picked up the phone. "Oh, hello, Aunty Vi. . ."

The children winked at each other as they tiptoed out. Aunty Vi would want to talk about the funeral, so Mum would be on the phone for ever.

It was cold out on the riverbank. Winter seemed to have arrived without them really noticing. Carla pulled her cardigan round her, wishing she'd remembered her coat. Woody wasn't bothered by the cold, but Penny was shivering, so Carla shouted at them to hurry up before they froze to death. All the river grass was drying up and going brown, making a dry whistling sound as the wind blew through it. The berries were red in the hedges and as the children hurried down the path they passed a twittering, rustling bush, as if hundreds of little birds were having a wild party in there.

"Getting ready to emigrate," said Woody.

"Migrate," corrected Carla.

"Sparrows don't migrate," said Penny. "They stay and shiver. The swallows went ages ago."

"Now look," said Carla, "I don't think I've made this clear. We are forbidden, under pain of death, to say anything about this to anyone. If it slips out, then the whole plan is sunk, and Grandpa ends up next to Grandma." Everyone thought about this. One of the most repeated tales about Grandma was how she made Mum eat an entire bowl of cold, burned cabbage soup, and then mop up her own sick afterwards. Another was how she'd told Dad on his wedding day that he'd never be good enough for her daughter. Their favourite story, though, was the time that Grandma had attacked

Grandpa's boat, *Julie*, with an axe in a fit of rage. The repairs were plain to see. After they'd heard this story (from old Barney who lived near the seashore) the children played at Grandma-with-an-axe for many weeks and pestered Grandpa for more detail, but all he'd say on the matter was, *"Never let an angry woman near an axe."*

A figure approached them on the river path. It was Mrs Davies, the founder member (and the worst cook) of the Baking Club. She was a small, thin woman with big green eyes which bulged out, like a frog's.

They hadn't seen her since Grandpa had died.

"Oh, children," she said, sweeping up. "We're all so sorry." She wore purple leggings over walking boots, and a bright yellow mackintosh buttoned up to her neck. "You found him?" She swivelled her eyes to Carla. "That must have been a shock." Her eyes were greedy for information.

"Yes," said Carla. She didn't want to talk about it.

"If there's anything I can do, *please* let me know."

"Yes," said Carla. Out of the corner of her eye she could see Woody looking miserable and Penny staring mutely at the water. She stuffed Penny's freezing hand into her big cardigan pocket and held it there, though Penny struggled a bit before she gave up. "We're in a rush. Sorry, Mrs Davies, we've got to go."

Mrs Davies nodded and let them past. "*Do* send my condolences to your parents."

"Why do people have to go on about it?" muttered

Woody, when they were safely out of earshot. "He's our grandpa."

Carla agreed. She wished everyone would leave them alone.

The barn smelled musty. Carla switched on the lights. Everything looked dusty and old. Leaves lay in little heaps all over the floor, they must have blown in under the door, and there was a large puddle on the floor where the skylight hadn't been shut properly and the rain had got in. Grandpa's heavy old brush stood in the corner. In her mind's eye Carla saw Grandpa pushing it across the floor, whistling. He'd sweep up at the end of every day. Carla heard snuffling and saw Woody leaning into *Valkyrie*, his arms covering his head. Penny was wandering around listlessly touching things. Of course, neither of them had been back here since Grandpa died. Carla hadn't thought of that. Maybe she was moving things on a bit too quickly.

"I keep expecting him to walk through the door," whispered Woody, and Carla went over and gave him a hug. She imagined he would push her away. But he didn't, not at first anyway.

"It's so strange," said Penny, picking up Grandpa's box of Christmas cards. He strung these up every year as Christmas decorations, he said, to look popular. He had instructed everyone not to give him any more Christmas cards as he still had these.

"*I may as well use the same ones,*" he always said.

"Unless I become deadly enemies with the sender, in which case I'll put it up anyway to spite them."

"Someone's going to have to clear all his stuff out," said Penny, putting down the box.

"Oh, don't," said Carla, not wanting to think about it. It was too final, too sad. "Let's look at *Valkyrie*."

"Grandpa was so proud of her," said Woody, running a finger over the stem. "Would he really want us to burn her?"

"It is a shame for her to be burned," admitted Carla. "But it will make the most beautiful funeral ever. Grandpa would get to go in her at least once."

"I'd like to have something to remember him by," said Woody stubbornly.

Carla felt cross. "Look, what do you suggest? Shall we just forget the whole plan and let him get buried? Or do we give him the send-off he really wants? It's his DREAM, for goodness' sake."

Woody picked up the tin of duck-egg paint and set it the right way up. "I know," he said. "It's still sad."

"Of course it is," said Carla shortly. "Our grandpa has died. I'm so miserable I want to run away and never come back." Her voice cracked and she turned away. She couldn't let herself get sad like this, she couldn't. There was too much to do.

After what seemed like ages, Penny spoke. "But how are we going to get to the sea?"

Carla lifted her head. She hadn't quite worked that part out yet. But surely there was a way.

"You're not going to make us row it down the Wich?" asked Penny, a note of alarm in her voice. "Only that would mean four funerals instead of just the one."

"Let's take it one step at a time," Carla said, not wanting to admit she had no plan for this bit yet.

Their river, the Dugg, flowed into the River Wich, a big, fast estuarine river, which went right out to sea. The River Wich had thick mud banks and a deadly current. The children were forbidden to row on it. Instead, Grandpa or Dad would load up the boats and canoes and take them out on the quiet waters and rhynes of the Somerset Levels, or they'd just mess about on the smaller River Dugg outside their house.

Penny walked the length of the boat. "Is it big enough?" she asked.

"How long is the coffin?" asked Woody. He frowned at Carla. "He is going to be in a coffin, isn't he? Only I. . ." His voice trailed away. He didn't have to say any more. Everybody felt the same way.

"He'll be in his coffin," said Carla briskly. "Anyway, we'll have to weight it, just in case it sinks before it burns properly."

Woody made a small noise in his throat. Carla thought he looked slightly sick.

"Maybe the chains would be useful for that," he said quietly, pointing to a heavy coil hanging from the beam.

"How do we make it burn properly?" asked Penny. "What if it's *raining*?"

Carla wondered again if she should stop the whole

thing now, before it got out of hand. "Look, we don't have to do it," she said. "It's a big job. It would be too much to ask any kid to arrange their own granddad's funeral, and we're planning something enormous." Her legs felt heavy, like the blood wasn't circulating properly. She wanted to go home and go to bed, to shut her eyes and sleep and forget about all of this. It was madness.

"But he'd love it," said Woody, taking a deep breath. "He'd think it was the best thing ever. If we take the thwarts out and lash the coffin to the safety harness, it should be secure."

Carla felt her spirits rise. "You've been thinking about this."

"I've done more than that," said Woody. "I worked out that in order to have any chance of launching *Valkyrie* off the beach, without drowning in the mud, we need to go on a spring tide or, failing that, the highest tide available." He grinned. "I looked on the calendar; the full moon is on Wednesday. . ."

"Which means the big spring tide is on Friday," said Carla. "The day before Grandpa's funeral."

"The current goes at seven knots on a spring tide," said Woody. "It would sweep an iron man on a steel boat out to sea."

A spluttering noise made them all jump.

"What was that?" yelped Woody. The noise came from behind a pile of fishing baskets Grandpa had stacked by the door.

"A cat?" mused Penny.

Carla felt terrified. It wasn't a cat. It was a person coughing. And whoever it was had heard everything.

It was all over before it had even begun.

An Idea

"Who's hiding?" shouted Woody. Carla and Penny exchanged glances. Woody usually avoided trouble whenever possible. He was, as Grandpa put it, *"A backstage man, not one for the limelight but still essential to the show."*

Grandpa said some odd things.

"You're trespassing," shouted Woody, bright red with anger. He marched over to the fishing baskets and pulled out a dark-haired boy. Carla recognized him. It was Ernie Blake. He was her age and he lived on a farm just outside the village. He went to a different school from the Moon children.

"Come to nose around, have you?" Woody looked ready to punch the boy. "Well, get out, this is PRIVATE PROPERTY."

"Calm down, Woody, it's only Ernie," said Carla. She glared at him. "But what are you doing here?"

Ernie drew himself up. "I'm sorry about your granddad," he said in a soft voice.

"So are we," said Carla flatly. How much had he heard? All of it?

"But Magnus – I mean, Mr Hughes – said we could build in his barn. Dad's bull escaped and now our cows are having Christmas calving a month early so we've been booted out of our building shed."

"What has this got to do with my grandpa's barn?" asked Carla icily.

Ernie looked at her like she was mad. "The carnival," he said, as if that should explain everything. "I'm the chairman of Sparks, the Little Wichley Carnival Club. Magnus said we could finish the build here, in his barn. The carnival's on Friday and we've got nowhere else to go. The cart will be along in a minute. Dad's bringing it behind his tractor."

Carla stared at him. Bigwich Carnival was the biggest, best carnival in the West Country, if not the world. She'd forgotten all about it. She felt a stab of alarm as she remembered that she was supposed to be Carnival Princess. Sophie, her best mate, had entered the pair of them in the competition for the role and, to both the girls' dismay, Carla had won. Naturally, in the last few days, none of the Moon family had given the carnival a thought. Their world had stopped. But it seemed everyone else was getting on with things as usual, as if this awful, awful thing hadn't happened.

"But Grandpa's died," said Carla. "Why did you think you could still build here?"

Ernie coughed. "I didn't think he'd mind," he said. Carla looked thunderous. "I didn't mean any disrespect. We just thought no one would really notice. We'll only be here for a few days, and then we'll be off."

Carla tried to think. It was maddening that anyone could come into Grandpa's barn and start *using* it, with Grandpa only dead two days. But she also had the beginnings of an idea. "What are you building this year?" she enquired.

Ernie looked sceptical. "You're not going to grass to the Sodbury Raiders, are you?"

"We're going to find out anyway if you're building in the barn," pointed out Carla.

"All right, it's a junior comic entry: *Bananas in Pyjamas*." Ernie watched their faces.

"That's terrible," said Penny.

"Maybe," said Ernie, leaning back against the wall, his thumbs in his jeans pocket. "But it wasn't my idea. I wanted *Frosty the Snowman*. You know, it would be, like, environmental. Polar bears wearing armbands and snowmen with sunglasses on. But everyone else thought *Frosty* was too political for carnival so they voted for *Bananas*. We've got the costumes made, but nobody wants to be a teddy bear."

Penny coughed. "Bigwich Carnival is Friday night, the day before Grandpa's funeral," she said.

There was a long pause. Carla was thinking hard.

There had to be some way they could turn this to their advantage.

"If you're dead set against it, we'll have to find somewhere else," said Ernie.

Carla breathed out. "No, wait. We'll arrange it so that you can build your entry in the barn." Woody opened and closed his mouth and Penny glared at her, but Carla ploughed on. "I'll clear it with Mum, but on one condition."

"What?" asked Ernie.

"You can't do *Bananas in Pyjamas*; you've got to do a Viking-themed tableaux. You can call it '*To Valhalla!*'."

"What's she on about?" Penny muttered to Woody.

"Valhalla," said Woody, "is the place where dead Viking heroes sail to. It's their heaven. Beautiful women called Valkyries help them to get there."

"Grandpa would definitely like that," said Penny.

Ernie sat on Grandpa's bench. "Look, I heard you talking. I hid because I felt awkward. So I heard all the stuff about burning *Valkyrie*." He looked carefully at Carla. "And I'm not sure if I heard the next bit right."

Carla said nothing. On one hand, Ernie and the Sparks could be a blessing in disguise, but on the other, things could spiral out of her control.

"Hey," said Ernie, "I liked your granddad. If you want to do what's right by him, then count me in."

Carla weighed up her options. If Ernie knew about their plan, then she may as well get some use out of him. "OK," she said. "You're in. But if you tell a soul about this, I'll get my friend who goes to your school to beat you up." Ernie flinched and Carla felt bad. She shouldn't go round threatening people. But she didn't know Ernie very well. "I won't really," she said, her voice softening. "It's just this is really important."

"I know," said Ernie. "Anyway, I wasn't scared. I'm a black belt in karate."

"I see," said Carla.

"Just kidding," said Ernie. "You'd better tell me what your plans are."

Carla glanced at the others and took a deep breath.

"We need to turn *Valkyrie* into a Viking ship," said Carla. "Because Grandpa wants a Viking funeral. If everyone thinks we're making a carnival display, no one will ask any questions. And we need to launch the boat on Friday because there's a strong tide and because the funeral is on Saturday."

"Carnival night is Friday," said Ernie. "How will that work?"

"Perfectly," said Carla, sounding more confident than she felt. "The whole town is crazy on carnival night. There must be an opportunity for us to slip away and give Grandpa his funeral." Her eyes lit up as she talked. "The boat will be loaded and ready to go."

Woody grinned. "Genius," he said.

"Madness," said Penny sourly. "How do we get hold of Grandpa? And who's going to drive the tractor and float to the sea?"

Ernie shrugged. "I've been driving tractors since I

was four years old," he said. "It will be no big deal, as long as I can somehow get Dad out of the frame." He sighed. "It's a cool idea. But we have to let the rest of the Sparks know. We'll need them."

"What?" Carla glared at him. "No way."

"We can't abandon *Bananas in Pyjamas*, build *To Valhalla!*, and then burn it, without letting them know why."

Carla frowned. "How many are there in Sparks?"

"Six, including me," said Ernie. "We're not a large club," he added.

"All kids?" asked Penny.

Ernie nodded. "All except my dad. He's going to pull the cart behind his tractor."

"Someone will tell," said Woody.

"Why should they?" asked Ernie.

Nobody answered.

"I want to meet everyone first," said Carla. "Then we'll decide. Don't say anything yet, Ernie."

"Sure." Ernie smiled. He had very dark eyes. Carla hoped he was as trustworthy as he looked.

"Just one thing," he said, looking round at them all. "Call me Ern."

Carla wandered off behind the tyre mountain to think about things. There were certainly a few big issues to sort out, but look at the progress already made. Yesterday Woody was on a starvation diet and bursting into tears every few seconds and Penny was shut in her room. Now Carla had definite team members, a ship, possible access to a tractor, a trailer and the beginnings of a plan. Her gaze fell upon Grandpa's leather bag of tools. It was old and dirty and rammed with knives and chisels and pliers and all sorts of other useful things. Grandpa said some of the tools were over a hundred years old. Carla pulled out a hammer and examined the worn wooden handle.

"We're going to give you your funeral, Grandpa, I promise," she whispered.

The clattering of an engine at the big side doors made them all jump. Grandpa had said these were cart doors which were used in the past for threshing machines to come into the barn. Grandpa usually kept them bolted shut.

"That'll be Dad and the Sparks," said Ern.

Carla and Woody heaved back the bolt and swung the doors open. A small grey tractor, hitched to a smallish trailer, sat outside. Mr Blake, Ern's dad, was a smiley man, with his son's dark eyes.

"Sorry about your grandpa, love," he said to Carla. "I'll be there at the church on Saturday to pay my respects. Now where can I put this trailer? Sorry for the inconvenience, but calving is more important than carnival. Least it is in my book, and the rest of my sheds are full."

Carla, glancing over at Ern, saw he'd put a finger to his lips.

They would have to do everything without Mr Blake guessing.

The Carnival Princess

Carla pressed her forehead against her bedroom window. It was six o'clock in the evening and so dark she couldn't see the river. She hated November. Everything was dead. She opened the window a crack and a freezing draught of air shot in. She listened to the rushing river and jumped when Dad called her for dinner. Dad was an electrical engineer and worked shifts at the power station three miles down the road at Sinkworthy. The children joked about his decontamination regime. When he arrived home, he'd leave his boots on the porch and go straight into the downstairs shower before he'd give anyone a kiss or have a cup of tea or anything.

"Is it because you're radioactive?" Penny asked him.

"No," he'd said. "It's because by the end of a shift I smell."

Carla wiped condensation from the window off her forehead. Her head was dancing with problems. She had worries piled up on worries. How to get hold of Grandpa? How to be sure the ride would take him? What if Mum found out? The complications were endless.

Then it was like Grandpa was speaking in her ear.

If you don't know how to do something, you may as well do it anyway. You might end up with surprising results. Look at me – when I was sixteen I went off to join agricultural college as I had a vague interest in cows: nice calm beasts. But I got lost and ended up in the recruitment office of the Royal Navy. I didn't come home for seven years. Mother went bananas. I was supposed to bring home fish and chips for supper.

"All right, Grandpa, I'll do it anyway," said Carla.

Downstairs, Mum was serving up dinner as Dad cleared his papers from the table. The kitchen was Carla's favourite place in the house. Dad had knocked through two rooms to make one. It was wide and long, with the stairs coming into it. A large wooden table took up one half of the room. Cupboard doors were painted different colours – Mum didn't like anything to match – and one wall was covered, floor to ceiling, with the children's and Mum's dodgy artwork. At the other end of the room was a log fire, a TV, a weary-looking sofa and an ancient armchair. Books were shelved on planks supported by bricks – Dad said he would get round to building proper shelves one day – and thick old walls kept out the cold.

"So scheme A would generate five per cent of the nation's electricity," Dad was saying, "and scheme B would generate two per cent, but it's far less expensive. . ." Dad was involved in a plan to design a turbine that generated electricity using the tides of the estuary. "What do you think?" he asked Mum.

"I think you should come and eat," said Mum.

"Five per cent doesn't seem very much," said Penny, drifting down the stairs.

"But that's five per cent of the entire nation's electricity supply," said Dad. "It's enormous."

"Five per cent is minuscule," said Penny. "No matter what it's five per cent of."

"If you're not sitting at the table in three seconds, Aurora gets the lot," snapped Mum. "Woody, turn off that television."

Dad winked at the children. "She's tired," he mouthed. Mum was always tired. She worked as a midwife in Bigwich and was often out all night and all weekend. But since Grandpa had died, she hadn't been to work at all. "They'll have to cope without me," she'd said.

"When's Maria due?" asked Carla, laying out knives and forks. Maria was Mum's oldest friend and had been trying to have a baby for over ten years. Then, just when she'd given up hope, she'd found out that she was expecting. Naturally she wanted Mum to be at the birth.

"Not for another three weeks," said Mum. Then she cleared her throat and told them how Grandpa was ready for visits if they wanted, at Mr Salt's Chapel of Rest.

"Do any of you want to go?" she asked.

No one said anything.

"Grandpa wouldn't mind if you didn't want to visit him," she said. "Don't feel pressured. I'm going tomorrow morning if anyone wants to come with me." She paused. "The funeral service will be at ten o'clock on Saturday. We'll all go to the undertakers' and then we'll be driven to the church in one of the posh black cars."

"Will we be going in a hearse?" asked Woody nervously.

"No, silly," said Mum. "It's a big black Mercedes."

"Cool," said Woody.

Dad sighed. "Magnus wouldn't have wanted a church service, Freya."

Everybody froze.

Mum glared at him. "What do you suggest?"

Dad shrugged. "I don't know. It just doesn't seem right. Magnus was a maverick, a free spirit. I doubt he ever set foot in a church in his life."

"He's in your wedding photos," pointed out Penny. "So that's at least once."

"Maybe this isn't the time to discuss it," said Mum. "Anyway, I've arranged it."

Carla toyed with her mashed potato. Since Grandpa

had died they'd been eating ready meals that were cooked in black plastic dishes. Penny said she liked them, but Woody wouldn't eat them at all.

"The Mercedes seats five passengers so we'll all be able to fit in," said Mum.

"What about Gus?" asked Dad.

Mum sighed. "Help me," she said to him. "They don't have bigger cars."

"Grandpa wasn't Gus's grandpa," said Penny. "So what does it matter?"

"No, Penny," said Mum. "Dad's right. Grandpa would have wanted Gus along with us."

"I'll go in a separate car, so Gus can travel with you," said Dad.

"I'd really like you by my side," said Mum, her voice wobbling. Everyone went quiet. Grandpa and Grandma only had one child, Mum, and she'd always been close to her dad. Carla knew that although Mum was organizing everything and holding the family together, she was devastated. Dad must have known this too; otherwise he'd have made more of a fuss about including Gus.

Gus.

He lived in a tiny maisonette in Bigwich. He was eighteen years old and did nothing apart from play computer games. He was also the children's half-brother. Dad had a baby with his girlfriend when he was only eighteen. Dad and the girlfriend split up and for a while Dad only saw Gus once a month. Then Dad met Freya and they married and had the three of them. When Gus was fourteen and Carla was nine, he'd come to live with them full-time. His mum had had enough of him and said it was time for his father to take responsibility.

It hadn't been easy for any of them. Gus was grouchy and unpredictable. He left his clothes and stuff lying around and would spend all his evenings and weekends lying on the sofa, hogging the telly. He used to drive Mum mad. He'd sneak down in the night and eat all the nice food. He'd even scoff all the snack bars Mum had stockpiled for the children's lunch boxes. He was lazy at school and never went out to any clubs or did any sports. He'd had awful spots and refused to take his trainers off, even though they *stank*. After Gus left school, everyone expected him to get a job. But he didn't. He just lay around the house, leaving sandwich crumbs everywhere. After nearly two years Dad said he'd had enough and sorted Gus out the place in Bigwich. Sometimes he came back for lunch on Sundays, and occasionally Carla would see him in town, but apart from that, they didn't bother each other. This suited Carla just fine. She'd never really liked Gus. He just seemed to cause trouble. And now he was gone, Mum had less work to do, and her parents didn't row about him.

It was easier now he wasn't around.

"We'll talk about it later," said Dad.

Woody scraped back his chair. "Can I go? I want to watch *Doctor Who*."

"Wait," said Mum. "This is important. You all need to know what's going to happen. There's the funeral on Saturday, and then a reception in the village hall afterwards."

Carla sighed. This was all so dreary and miserable, and so unlike what Grandpa would have wanted. She felt a fresh resolve that she was doing the right thing.

"It's a shame we couldn't do something more exciting for Magnus," said Dad. Carla thought he must have been reading her mind. "I bet he'd like his ashes fired up to space in a rocket or something," he went on.

Carla dropped her knife. It clattered to the floor.

Mum sighed. "If you'd like to organize it, Kit, then go ahead. You're the engineer."

Carla gazed at her father thoughtfully. Was there any way she could involve him? What would he say if she told him what they were planning? Carla caught sight of Penny watching her. Her sister was shaking her head and mouthing, "NO." Penny was probably right. What if Dad put a stop to the whole thing?

After tea, Woody and Penny slunk away and Mum was straight on the phone. Dad was folding washing. Carla thought it was a good time to bring up the subject of the Sparks. "Oh, we know about that already," said Dad, folding Woody's school trousers. "Mr Blake cleared it with us yesterday. I meant to tell you."

"We've decided to join," said Carla, wondering how he would react.

Dad looked up from a pile of odd socks. "But the carnival is on Friday," he said. "It's the night before Grandpa's funeral. Your mother might think it was inappropriate."

Maybe not as inappropriate as stealing Grandpa's body, Carla thought darkly, and pushing him out to sea in a burning boat.

"Talk to Mum," said Dad. "It might be strange for you to be leaping around on a carnival float one day and going to your grandpa's funeral the next." He dropped a sock and bent to scoop it up. "And you're this year's princess. I'd completely forgotten."

Carla grunted. "Don't remind me." She really, really did not want to be Carnival Princess. She'd only entered because Sophie, her best mate, had badgered her. They'd both filled in application forms and sent off their photographs. Carla never thought she'd win the horrible thing. She'd even given herself a crazy hairstyle for the *Gazette* photographs to ensure she lost votes. But she'd won. And now she was expected to parade on a float around Bigwich for three hours in the freezing cold. And then she was supposed to do the rounds of the other towns for every weekend nearly up till Christmas.

"It is the curse of beauty," Penny had said when she'd heard. "I'm glad I'm average-looking and will never be paraded like a doll." Woody had laughed so hard he'd got the hiccups. And as for Grandpa, he'd just said, "*Soak up the glory. If you don't, we will.*"

But Carla had only done it for Sophie. And now

Sophie was being funny about it. Mum said she was probably a bit jealous, because she'd wanted to win herself. Carla had tried so hard not to win. She'd put her interests down as "worm catching" and "eating mud pie", because she was sure that would lose her a few votes. But apparently people had voted for her because of her "witty personality".

Rats!

"Maybe they'll let me off," said Carla hopefully, "because of Grandpa."

"I'm sure they would," said Dad. "But how are the organizers going to find another princess in time?"

Carla shrugged. Surely it wouldn't be too hard? She was ambivalent, but wouldn't most normal girls kill for this glory?

"I thought you said you were joining the Sparks," said Dad. "You can't be in two places at once." Carla stared at the odd socks as an idea took shape in her head. Maybe there *was* a way of being in two places at once.

Gundy Beach

Monday morning was dry and mild. Dad was pulling up dead plants in the vegetable patch, and Mum had gone to meet the caterers about the funeral lunch, so the children had some time to themselves. Woody was supposed to go fossil collecting with his mate at Kilve Beach, but had cancelled. "Me and Benji usually spend all our time laughing," he said. "But I don't feel like it. And if we don't laugh, what else are we going to do?"

"Let's cycle out to the bird hide and have a meeting," Carla said. "We won't be overheard there." She also reckoned it would also be a good opportunity to have a reconnaissance of Gundy beach.

Penny swiped a packet of ginger cake from the cupboard.

"Mum wouldn't notice if I was wearing a monkey suit

at the moment," she whispered, shoving the cake into her rucksack.

Dad appeared as the children wheeled their bicycles out of the gate.

"Where are you going?"

"To the hide," said Carla. "Then we're calling in at the barn to meet the Sparks."

"Don't go out on the mudflats," warned Dad. "The tides are very strong and fast at this time of year."

"We won't," sang Penny.

Dad nodded. "Just be sensible."

"Aren't I always?" Carla pedalled away, crunching into gear.

The children were puffing and blowing as they raced up the river path, only stopping to lift their bicycles though the gates where the River Dugg joined the Wich estuary. The tide was pouring in over the thick, shining mud. A shard of sunlight broke through the clouds and the whole river sparkled. They watched a heron take off from the water. Here the estuary was so broad that the sheep on the far bank were just dots. They left the estuary path and cycled over a damp field to a tall wooden structure. It was a hide, built for people to observe the birds and wildlife of the estuary. The children left their bicycles at the bottom and climbed the creaking wooden steps.

"I'd forgotten how steep it is," complained Penny. Her cheeks were pink.

Carla realized that this crazy plan of theirs, possibly doomed to fail, was at least getting Penny out of her bedroom. She watched as Woody flung the rucksack on the floor and dived in, looking for the cake. If they weren't here, he'd also be moping at home, and not eating. Maybe she was doing the right thing after all. But it was hard to know. She was the eldest and, when the crunch came, she'd have to take responsibility.

The Gundy peninsula lay between Greenham-on-Sea and Sinkworthy Flats. At low tide, the shore was slick with mud and rammed with birds and wildlife. The battery box of Sinkworthy nuclear power station, where Dad worked, loomed on the horizon. On the other side of the bay stood Iron Knoll, a vast, flat-topped hill and ancient fort. Standing on the top platform of the hide, Carla could see the stretch of beach where she planned to launch Grandpa. The coast road ran parallel to a line of dunes. Beyond these was a flat expanse of sand and shingle. Seaweed marked the high water line and the beginning of the mud fields. Something was glinting in the mud at the far end of the shore. Carla screwed up her eyes. She couldn't work out what it was. It looked like a large metal box. She looked over the channel at Wales: a vast dark mound, punctuated with smoking chimney stacks and tiny boats.

The hide always made Carla think of a tower. It was square, with salt-smeared windows on all sides. The wood creaked in the wind. Battered laminated posters featuring estuarine birds and wildlife were pinned to the walls. The children sat at the bench facing the big window which looked out over the bay.

Carla got out her notebook. She'd made a list of everything she could think of that they needed to sort out.

Tide times
Transport
Getting Grandpa of out Mr Salt's
Flammable stuff (paraffin?)
Outboard motor?
Attaching coffin to boat
Little Wichley Sparks CC. What to tell
Aftermath

"There needs to be more on that list," said Penny.

"Such as?" Carla was worried. Hadn't they got enough to deal with?

"Like how can you be Carnival Princess and be on the *To Valhalla!* float at the same time? And how are we going to get away from Bigwich, through the crowds and reach the sea?"

"That's under transport," said Carla crossly. "You're just making things complicated." She handed round some more cake. She knew from experience that if she wanted her siblings to stay focused, they had to eat regularly. Also she hoped it would be a distraction from the question. She was still trying to work out how she could be in two places at once.

"What does aftermath mean?" asked Woody. Carla looked out to sea. This was the point she dreaded most of all. Every time she thought about it, she felt a black hole widen in her insides. But if she was going to rope her brother and sister into this, it was only fair that they should know the risks. "If we take Grandpa from Mr Salt's," she began, "well, that's *body snatching*. If we were grown-ups, we'd get put in prison."

"But we're not stealing him, he's ours," pointed out Penny.

Carla wasn't sure about this; she liked the sound of it, but it was hardly the only issue. "Even if the police don't get involved, what do you think Mum is going to say when they find Grandpa is missing? She's going to go insane! She'll be so sad and worried. And if she finds out we're behind it, she might hate us for ever." Carla bit her lip. She was talking herself, and probably the others, out of the whole thing. The other two were quiet. Could she ask them to risk everything? Carla wasn't sure she should even be talking to Penny about this stuff. She was only nine. Maybe she shouldn't be thinking about dead bodies and how to steal them.

But Penny was unperturbed. "Why don't we take Grandpa, but leave his coffin? We could put something heavy in it, so everyone would think he was still there," she suggested.

"Oh no," interrupted Carla. "We're leaving him in his coffin." She didn't want anyone messing around with him.

"In that case we need a substitute," said Penny briskly. "We need an identical coffin to Grandpa's, and we need to put something that weighs the same as Grandpa."

"Mum said we could go visit Grandpa tomorrow morning," said Woody. "We could check out his coffin then."

"But how are we going to get one the same?" said Carla, looking at her siblings in surprise. These were great ideas.

"You can get anything on the internet," said Woody.

"But not a coffin, and not in five days." But Carla could see the possibilities. Maybe there was a way to do this without getting into horrendous trouble after all.

"What does a coffin cost, anyway?" asked Woody.

"Thousands of pounds, I expect," said Carla. "They have all that shiny wood, and silky stuff inside, and all the metal fittings and things."

"You seem to know an awful lot about it," said Penny.

"I only know from watching *Dracula*," said Carla, realizing this wasn't the best source of information.

"What about a cardboard coffin?" suggested Woody brightly. "Grandpa would like that. He's always on about not making a fuss."

"It would be eco-friendly," said Penny.

"I don't know if he's even in a coffin yet," said Carla. She pictured Grandpa lying curled up on his couch in his barn and her eyes welled with tears. A vivid memory came into her mind. It was the first time Grandpa had taken her out on the river. Mum had got her wrapped up in a special tiny life jacket.

"Look after my daughter," Mum had shouted, white-faced, from the bank. Carla remembered sitting squarely in the centre of the boat as Grandpa rowed them up the River Dugg, pointing out birds and flowers. She remembered lying back and looking up at the sky. Then she remembered a splash of wet on her cheek as Grandpa drew in the oars and let them just drift, drift down the river.

He sang as the boat bobbed in the current.

"The sweetest girl I ever saw

Sat sucking cider through a straw. . ."

Of course, since then they'd been out with Grandpa hundreds of times. He'd taught all of them to row *Julie* up and down the River Dugg. He'd not taken them sailing in her; he said she was too hard to handle and the bay was too dangerous. But on the few nights when Mum and Dad were away and Grandpa was looking after them, he'd left Penny sleeping soundly in her bed and taken Carla and Woody downstream to catch elvers or dip netting for salmon.

"There's nothing better than a good eel pie," Grandpa said. *"Only for God's sake don't tell your mother where we got them."*

Julie was an old boat. Grandpa had owned her for years. When the children had moved into the cottage just along the bank from him, he said they could mess about in her, on condition that they always took an adult with them. Now *Julie* was moored to the small jetty on the bank, just outside Grandpa's garden. Her mast stood in a corner of Grandpa's barn and her sails and rigging were stuffed under his couch. *Julie*'s dark green paint was cracking and there was always a puddle of bilge sloshing about in the bottom. Grandpa said she wasn't leaking, it was rainwater, but even so, he was very particular about life jackets. Grandpa said that unless someone could swim, they should never go out on the water.

"When I was a seaman, there was this auxiliary-man who fell in the sea. We were in calm waters off the Brittany coast. We threw him a line, but he sank without trace. The idiot couldn't swim. Imagine being in the Royal Navy and not being able to swim! Mind you, he'd been at the grog so that couldn't have helped."

"Look at that." Penny jumped to her feet and pressed her face to the window. "It's a car."

Carla looked. Penny was pointing at the funny metal box thing she'd spotted earlier. Her sister was right. It was a car, half-buried in the mud.

"It must have got trapped by the tide," said Woody. "Strange we didn't hear about it."

Quite often lads from Bigwich would come and drive their cars up and down the beach, scarpering long before anyone called the police.

Carla shivered. "I hope they got out," she said.

It was plain to her now that she was looking at the

roof of the car; it must have sunk so deep no one could pull it out.

"Another victim of the Gundy Bay tides," said Penny brightly. "I hope we're not next."

There was a short silence. Carla dragged her eyes away from the car. She decided they'd launch Grandpa further up the beach. She'd have to think very carefully about what to do about the mud.

Woody kicked his feet against the wall. "I've been thinking. What if Grandpa ends up in Wales?" He peered at the dark smoking chimneys and stacks of Newport across the channel. "He might wash up on the other side."

"Or in Ireland," said Penny.

"We're not just going to push him out to sea to drift around, we're going to cremate him," said Carla crossly. "Besides, we're going to weight him down. Anything that doesn't burn is going to sink." The children stared out to sea. Although the tide was coming in, the water was still just a grey-silver strip in the distance beyond the acres of mud.

Carla went back to her list. "I'll tell you my rough plan for transporting Grandpa to the sea." She lowered her voice. "But I'll need to clear it with Ern. . ."

Sometime later, feeling slightly sick from too much cake, the children climbed down. Sandbags were piled around the foot of the hide, probably to keep out the wet, Carla supposed.

"Woody," she said, "would one of those sandbags fit in your pannier?"

Woody eyed them up. "Yes, but it might buckle my wheels. Why?"

"I'll tell you later," said Carla. She had an idea but didn't want to give too much information to her brother and sister just yet. They might be a bit squeamish about what she had in mind. Anyway, she doubted whether the bags by the hide were enough for what she had in mind. Woody tried to pick up one of the bags. He went bright red under the effort as he hauled it up to his chin.

"Blimey!" he said. "It's a dead weight."

"Exactly," said Carla.

Sparks

There were five Sparks including Ern.

"Samantha, Isla, Bullet and Jimmy," introduced Ern. The Moon children knew most of them already. At fifteen, Samantha Jackson was in the year above Carla at school. Samantha had a round face and was a relaxed, smiling sort of person, so Carla wasn't worried about her bossing everyone around – that was going to be *her* job. Isla Godfrey was twelve and very thin with long hair down to her waist. She was in the same class as Woody. Bullet was small and serious-looking. At eight, he was the youngest Spark. He wore clean white trainers and a navy shirt with an orange and brown striped tank top. His real name was Gurpal Sudra but he said he preferred Bullet. His dad was also an engineer at Sinkworthy Point. Jimmy Patterson was nine and dressed in a boiler suit and dirty black wellies. "And I'd like to be known as Ratsy," he said.

"That's new," said Ern.

Jimmy shrugged. "I've never liked Jimmy."

"But why Ratsy? asked Isla. "Why not Ziggy or Mr Cool or something?"

"Rats are clever and sly," said Jimmy. "Like me."

"They're also vermin," muttered Penny. Carla coughed. She wasn't sure how she was going to proceed. She had a half-baked plan to tell them a story about how one of the judges was really into Vikings and that if they went as *To Valhalla!* they were sure to win a trophy or two. Either that or she was going to tell them a barefaced lie that she KNEW for a fact that there was another carnival club doing *Bananas in Pyjamas*. She breathed in, breathed out, and breathed in again. She was going to lie to all these kids. She really was. Any second. She caught a glimpse of a furry yellow costume hanging out of Samantha's bag. Carla tried to kid herself she was doing everyone a favour. They were going to be a laughing stock if they carried on with *Bananas in Pyjamas*.

"We're sorry your granddad died," piped up Bullet.

Carla stared at him. "Thanks." Woody kept his gaze firmly fixed to the ground and Penny was standing still, as white as a sheet.

"He was pretty cool," said Samantha.

"And it was so nice of him to let us use his barn," said Isla through a mouthful of hair. "And we're all up for *To Valhalla!*"

Carla shot a furious look at Ern. "What did you say?"

"*Bananas* wasn't shaping up," said Isla. She spat out her hair. "We'd come to a dead end. This will give us some focus. Ern's talked it all through with us."

"But the carnival is on Friday, and you've done all this work," spluttered Carla.

"Hey, don't talk us out of it," said Samantha. "I'm excited about wearing a toga and waving my sword."

"Toga?" Penny gave Carla an incredulous look.

"We love the idea of using the boat," said Bullet. "And we can use the same lights that we built for *Bananas*. And the generator is finally working. Also, Mr Blake says *Valkyrie* will fit on his trailer with room to spare. So let's go for it."

Carla nodded dumbly.

"OK," said Isla. "I've been researching Viking ships. There's both archaeological and written evidence. I've been looking at the great sagas and some museum reports."

Carla glanced at Woody. Was all this getting out of her control or was everything fine?

Ern touched her shoulder. "Chill," he whispered. "She's cool."

"It's nice to have some background," said Isla. "I've got a picture of a recovered Viking ship burial. It's in a museum in Norway. The ship is huge and beautiful. It's called the Oseberg ship." She opened a file and passed Carla the picture. Carla was looking at an ancient vessel made of dark wood. The front curved up into a spiral and was decorated with intricately carved flowers and leaves and animals.

"We can't make that in five days."

"You don't say," muttered Penny.

"We can make a good attempt at recreating a Viking ship using *Valkyrie*," said Isla. "Though I suggest we make a dragon figure head for the front of the ship rather than the curved stem. Some of us could be Norse gods and the rest could be oarsmen, sitting down and pretending to row. Why did he call his boat *Valkyrie* anyway?"

The Moon children looked at each other.

"Grandpa always said he had Viking blood," said Carla. "He said his ancestors sailed over and landed at Watchet. They raided the royal silver mint. He said his great-great-great-great-great-great-great-great-great . . . how many more?" she asked Penny.

"Maybe six more greats," Penny answered. She'd been counting on her fingers.

"Anyway, he said his ancestor got drunk, fell over a dead sheep, was knocked unconscious and got left behind. Grandpa said this bloke then had to blend in with locals so they didn't kill him in revenge for all the looting. Apparently he blended in so well he ended up marrying a local girl and staying put."

"Is this true?" asked Isla.

Carla shrugged. "It's one of Grandpa's favourite stories. It may as well be true. He says his family have been trying to fit in ever since."

She felt a bit funny saying all this family stuff to these strangers, but everyone was listening intently.

"I knew there would be something. People always choose meaningful names for their boats," said Isla. "We're going to need a dragon's head and neck. It should be easy enough with cardboard, chicken wire, papier mâché and some gold spray. Anyone want to start? It should be about three metres tall."

"I'll do it," said Samantha.

"And reports say that the Viking longships had striped and colourful sails. Are we going to do sails?" asked Isla.

"*Valkyrie* is a sailing boat," said Woody. "But a very simple one. She has two sails, the spritsail and the foresail. It's easy to take the whole lot down. The mast is unstayed, you see, and the sprit loops through the snotter and—"

"What colour are these sails?" interrupted Bullet.

"Off-white," said Woody.

"We need to look good at the carnival," said Bullet, "so we need to brighten them up." An earnest discussion broke out, debating the merits of striped sails versus the five-day deadline.

"So we'll keep the sails as they are, but with bunting," concluded Bullet. Carla frowned. Everything was moving too quickly for her. But Woody was already helping Ratsy do something with newspaper, and Isla and Samantha had broken off into a discussion about how to attach the figurehead to the boat. Even sceptical

Penny had got out a notepad and was writing down ideas. Ern and Bullet were now discussing bunting. The barn bustled and buzzed. The place was lit by two narrow strip lights, which hung from the rafters and were not very bright. It was cold because no one thought to light the burner. The children's breath clouded out around them.

Carla wasn't doing anything. She knew there were some major problems she hadn't sorted yet, but at least things were happening. She watched Ern lean into the boat, pointing out something to Bullet.

If he didn't keep their secret, they were finished.

Mr Salt's Funeral Parlour

"**C**ome on," said Mum, gripping Carla's hand and leading her up a narrow, cobbled street. "Let's do this, if you're sure?"

"It's all right," said Carla. "I found him, remember?" She squeezed her mother's hand. "Let's go and see Grandpa." She was calm for her mother's sake, but really she felt sick. The others hadn't wanted to come. They were spending the morning with the Sparks, turning *Valkyrie* into a Viking boat for a carnival parade.

The funeral-parlour building was smaller than Carla expected. And as they stepped into the reception, her stomach tightened. But it wasn't scary; it was just a room with a massive aquarium swimming with colourful fish. Tasteful flower pictures hung on the wall.

Double doors were propped open, leading to a big corridor with several doors leading off it.

"Mrs Moon?"

A woman sat at the reception desk. She was wearing a light green jumper. Carla was glad she wasn't dressed in black.

"I'm Annabel," she said. "You've come to see your father. He's all ready for you. Would you like a cup of tea first?"

Mum nodded, and despite everything Carla felt a smile inside. She had never, ever known her mother to refuse a cup of tea. Even, such as now, in moments of Great Crisis. They sat on comfy chairs and waited for Annabel to return.

"Funny kind of job," whispered Mum.

"The opposite of yours," whispered back Carla. They heard a car engine die outside. A door slammed. Annabel returned and presented Mum with a cup of steaming tea. Carla wondered how many sad people had drunk from that cup.

"Squash?" Annabel asked Carla brightly.

"No, thanks," said Carla stiffly. At thirteen she was too old to be automatically offered squash instead of tea.

"That's good," said Mum, swallowing a slug of the hot liquid. Carla thought again how tired her mother was looking. She'd not noticed the grey hairs at her temples before, or how her eyes looked closer together. In fact, Mum didn't really look like Mum at all. Carla noticed she had a yellowish stain on the knee of her trousers and her collar wasn't turned out properly. Carla gave her mother's hand another squeeze. But the movement must have surprised her because she slopped hot tea all over her legs.

"Ow, Carla, look what you're doing, ow ow ow!" yelled Mum. Carla shrank back in her seat. "Ow," said Mum again. Carla saw a tear plop out from her mother's eye and land on the table.

"Sorry," said Carla as Mum tried to wipe her legs. Annabel passed over a box of tissues. Each tissue had flowers printed on them. Carla supposed all this stuff was supposed to cheer people up. Cups of tea, flowery tissues. But nothing helped really, did it? Nothing was going to bring Grandpa back.

"It's a stressful time," Annabel said kindly.

"Indeed," said Mum in a strained voice. She looked at Annabel. "Is there a loo?"

"Just there, on the right. Take your time," said Annabel.

"Are you OK here?" muttered Mum, not meeting Carla's eye.

"Go, Mum, I'll be fine," said Carla. She could see that her mother needed to be on her own for a little while. Mum pushed back her chair so hard it fell over. "Oh damn," she said. She looked aghast. "Sorry."

"I'll get the chair," said Annabel soothingly. "You go." Carla sat and stared at the table as they listened to the ladies' door slam. The hand dryer blasted on, and over it came the unmistakable sound of Mum weeping.

"Don't worry," said Annabel. "Everybody cries. It's normal. We get through about one hundred boxes of tissues a week." Carla tried to smile back but couldn't. This is as bad as it gets, she thought, listening to the muddled sobs coming through the wall. When Mum finally came out of the loo her eyes were redder than ever and her eye make-up had smudged. Mum had attempted to wipe the worst of it off, but this had resulted in two dark circles under her eyes.

"Right," she said to Annabel. "I'm ready." She looked at Carla. "You OK?"

Carla nodded, feeling anything but.

Grandpa lay in a wooden coffin in the middle of a small, dimly lit room. There was a large wooden crucifix on the wall and some chairs dotted round the room. Mum's hand shook as she touched his cheek. Carla couldn't work out what was wrong with him. Then she realized someone had styled his hair and given him a middle parting. Grandpa never brushed his hair.

"Hello, Dad," whispered Mum, and Carla had to look away. There was a pressure in her throat making her breathe funny. She didn't like the carpet. It was pinkish with a white hexagonal pattern. It made her eyes blurry.

"You were a lovely dad," whispered Mum, stroking his hair.

"And a lovely grandpa," said Carla stoutly. She made herself look at his face, so familiar, but so different. So still. He was really gone. She steadied herself on the back of a chair and looked at his closed eyes and thought of the twinkle that was usually behind them.

"You all have your mother in you. But Woody is most like her. Penny is like your dad, and you, Carla, you're most like me, I think."

"But I've got brown eyes and you've got blue," said Carla.

"I don't mean what we look like; you're the spit of Freya. I mean what goes on in your head. I think sometimes we share a similar way of seeing the world. You're also stubborn, devious and single-minded. Just like me."

The idea that she was like Grandpa made Carla feel strong. It meant he would approve of what she was doing. But she wasn't sure about devious. That sounded too much like Grandma.

"But what was she really like?" Carla had asked him once, when they were out rowing on the levels. Grandpa had sat back, put the oars in their brackets and looked up to the sky. He'd sighed.

"She was a strong woman, but kindness wasn't one of her gifts. Don't repeat that. Maybe I wasn't a very good husband. She would have been happier with someone else, I think. But in those days nobody got divorced if they somehow ended up with the wrong person. But I think, on balance, we made the best of it. And I'll never ever regret it, because we had Freya, and I wouldn't swap her for the world."

Carla had heard that dead people just looked asleep. Carla wasn't sure about that. Grandpa just looked dead. She shut her eyes; it was hard to look at him. So hard. This couldn't be her lovely grandpa.

But he was still here, of course, that was the beauty of it. He was here inside her head, talking to her.

"Are we doing the right thing, Grandpa?" she asked him silently.

The answer came back immediately.

"Of course you are. But for goodness' sake, don't go putting yourself or anyone else at risk."

"I'm still not sure, Grandpa. And I haven't really got a proper plan. I'm just making it up as I go along."

"You put one foot in front of the other, and things will work out. Just keep going. You're doing great. Carla, sweetheart, let your mum have some time alone with me, will you?"

"OK, Grandpa."

"I'm just popping out for a minute," Carla told her mother, who nodded, barely seeming to hear her. Carla stepped out of the room, breathed out and scanned the hall. Annabel wasn't at her desk. There were three doors apart the ones for the loos and the chapel of rest. All three doors were marked PRIVATE. Carla knew that Grandpa wasn't usually kept in the chapel of rest. They'd just put him there for their visit. Carla needed to know where Grandpa was kept the rest of the time. She had a couple of ideas about how to get him out. One was to somehow sneak in and hide somewhere, wait until all the staff had gone home. No one would expect someone to break *out* of this place. Her other idea was much more risky and she didn't think she could do it. It involved talking to Mr Salt, the funeral director. He was an old friend of Grandpa's and maybe, just maybe, he would turn a blind eye if something a little strange took place.

Crossing the hall to the window, Carla looked outside and saw Annabel in the courtyard. She was deep in conversation with a short man and was smoothing back her hair and showing lots of teeth. Carla held her breath as she crept down the hall to the reception area. She stepped round to Annabel's side of the desk and slid open the top drawer. Her hands were sweating as she searched, but it was full of papers, nothing more. She didn't know exactly what she was looking for but hoped for something like the instructions for disabling the alarm, or a key, a code, or SOMETHING. There was nothing of any use in the next drawer either, just a stack of cards advertising funeral cortèges: you could take your loved one to their funeral in a carriage pulled by four black horses with black feathers in their headbands or, if you preferred, you could transport the deceased in a black shiny motorcycle sidecar. Carla thought it was all creepy. The third drawer was locked.

She tried the door next to the fish tank. NO ADMITTANCE. She had her story straight. If anyone asked, she'd got lost. The door opened with a nasty little whine. She stepped into the dark room and fumbled along the wall for the switch. When the lights flickered on she stepped back smartly. There were rows of coffins propped up on their ends and leaning into each other. There must have been at least thirty of them. They were all brown and wooden, with brass handles, just like Grandpa's. Only these had their lids.

And here was Grandpa's lid, propped up by the door.

Magnus Michael Hughes

Carla furiously rubbed away the prickling tears.

"Sometimes answers come out of the blue. But you have to keep your eyes open to find them."

Carla touched the nearest coffin. The wood was smooth and cool. She gave it a gentle push to test the weight, and to her alarm it swayed and she had to grab the other side to stop it toppling right over. She had to strain and push to get the coffin standing upright again. She stood back, panting. One thing was sure, when it came to moving Grandpa: she was going to need some help. She opened the door and peeped out. She tiptoed into reception and, before she completely bottled out, hurried down the corridor, past the chapel of rest, past the loos and stopped at the door right at the end. It had a very large sign. STRICTLY PRIVATE.

Carla eyed the sign for a few seconds. Was she brave enough to go through? She wasn't sure if she could hold her nerve much longer. But this was for Grandpa. Nothing else mattered.

The door made a swishing noise when Carla pushed it open. It was heavy, like a fire door. She peeked into a large bright room, with the walls painted white and red tiles on the floor. Bare steel tables lined the walls. There was also a set of three metal sinks and a large dispenser of pink liquid soap. An electronic lifting trolley sat in one corner. A frosted-glass door with an alarm pad above it gave access to the courtyard. And there was something else. An enormous stainless-steel fridge took up one whole wall. There were labels stuck to the doors at intervals. Some were blank, others were not. Carla read through the names.

Halley Grey
Oswald Hooper

And there was his.

Magnus Hughes

This was where they stored Grandpa. Carla stared at his name, rubbing her cheek. This was all so strange, so surreal. She felt like she was in a bubble. She had to look away.

Through the thick frosted glass of the door Carla could see Annabel, leaning back against the hearse and waving her arms around, engrossed in chat. Carla supposed it must get pretty lonely in here, especially on your own, with only dead people for company. It all made Carla feel glad to be alive. She told herself she was going to relish every single minute of her life. Carla examined the door, trying to work out how the lock worked, when the door from the corridor suddenly swung open.

"Can I help you?" said a surprised voice.

Rowan

A tall, familiar-looking young man with dark hair stared at her. Carla was so horrified at being caught she couldn't spit out her speech about being lost. The only word that came out was "Sorry".

"It's supposed to be private in here," he said. Carla waited for the explosion. But the man didn't seem fazed by her. In fact, he appeared to be amused. "I know you," he said. Carla said nothing. It was safer. The man leaned back against a stainless-steel sink and rubbed his chin thoughtfully. He needed a shave. "You're Gus Moon's little sister," he said. "You are either Penny or Carla. No, you're the big one; you're Carla." Carla felt her cheeks heat up. That was weird, being described as Gus's little sister. She'd never really thought of him as her brother. Gus wasn't like Woody.

"I'm Rowan," said the stranger. "I work here. What

are you doing in the prep room? I put your grandpa in the chapel of rest half an hour ago."

Carla liked the way he was so matter-of-fact. He seemed normal. She would have thought that someone who worked in a place like this would have been pretty strange. She remembered him now. She'd seen him at Gus's once or twice, and he may have even been to their house, years ago.

"Don't worry – we're looking after your grandpa," said Rowan. "I knew Magnus, you know. He used to take me and Gus out in *Julie*. We nearly got caught poaching by the river police once. It was the most exciting night of my life. And he took us to see the bore on a spring tide. Have you seen it?"

Carla nodded. A few years ago there was the highest tide for years, and Grandpa had made her and Woody (Penny was too small) get up at four o'clock in the morning to watch the bore pile down the river, a wall of muddy water like a mini tsunami.

"Never underestimate the sea. It is full of tricks and surprises."

"He paid me for the elvers I caught," said Rowan. "It was the first money I'd ever earned. What *are* you doing in here, by the way?"

Carla hesitated, weighing him up. She liked him. He could be a valuable ally. But he was Gus's friend and anyway, he almost certainly wouldn't risk his job for her.

"I got lost," she said, and had to look away.

"You'd better try and locate your way back to your mum. I expect she's wondering where you are." Rowan washed his hands. "And I've got work to do."

Carla hurriedly backed away. "I'll leave you to it," she muttered.

Rowan laughed. "Don't worry; I'm just vacuuming the hearse. And I'll look after your grandpa, OK? I had to bury my gran about a year ago. I know how it feels to lose someone you love." Carla nodded dumbly. She really had to find her mother before someone less friendly than Rowan came along, or worse, before someone dead was carried in.

"Give me a call any time if you want to know anything or if you need any help with anything," said Rowan, opening a cupboard and bringing out a vacuum cleaner. Carla opened the door, but let it fall shut again. Annabel was back at her desk. If Carla walked out, Annabel would know that she had been in the preparation room. Not good. Not good at all.

"Is Annabel out there?" asked Rowan, reading her thoughts. Carla nodded dumbly. How was she going to get out of this? "I'll let you out the other way," said Rowan. "Then you can walk in the main entrance. You can say you slipped out for some fresh air." He walked over to the exit and opened a grey panel mounted on the wall. Then he scratched his head. "I always forget the alarm code," he said. "I'm rubbish with numbers."

Carla held her breath.

"I know there's a two in it," he muttered. "But is it

second or third?" He punched in four numbers and then unlocked the door. "All clear." He smiled. "See you around. But maybe not in here again, hey? Though it's nice to have a visitor, especially one with a beating heart."

Carla nodded and fled outside, cheeks burning.

3287.

That was the security code for the door. She'd memorized every number that Rowan had punched in.

Carla skirted round the hearse and walked in through the main door. Annabel looked up from her desk and a frown wrinkled her forehead. Then she smiled.

"Are you going back in, dear?"

Carla nodded. This was all working out! It was going to be easy, easy, easy! Grandpa would have loved all this.

"Sometimes you have to step out of the real world to get the right things done."

"This is all pretty unreal, Grandpa."

"You're doing brilliantly, darling."

Carla stepped into the chapel of rest.

"Hello, beautiful," said Mum, looking up and giving her a big smile. "I've been chatting to Grandpa."

"And so have I," said Carla.

What About Gus?

Back at home and holed up in her bedroom, Carla decided not to tell the others *everything* she'd found out. It might be too much information for them to deal with, especially the stuff about the fridge. But she did tell them about the security code. "I need to think it through," she told them, "but I think we'll be able to get Grandpa out of there. What have you been doing?"

"Reading *Beowolf*," said Woody, swinging his legs as he sat on the window seat. "It's all about Vikings, I think – it's pretty hard to understand. There's this monster, right, and it goes around eating everyone and—"

"What's this got to do with Grandpa?" interrupted Penny. "Who cares about monsters?"

"Shut up, Penny," said Carla. "Carry on Woody." She knew her brother was cross because the tips of his ears were white. Woody glared at Penny and continued. "A thane called Weohstan (I'm not sure how you say it) killed a murderous dragon, but then *he* was killed in the process. In the story there's a description of his funeral."

"The dragon's or Weo what's-his-name's?" muttered Penny.

"Both," said Woody firmly. "In this story, he didn't get sent out to sea. Weohstan was put on a funeral pyre. The women sang a sad song called a dirge as their hero was burned away to ashes." Woody leafed through a tatty paperback and then read out an extract.

"The warriors began to rouse on the barrow the greatest of funeral fires; the wood-reek mounted up dark above the smoking glow, the crackling flame, mingled with the cry of the weeping – the tumult of the winds ceased – until it had consumed the body, hot to the heart."

"Mum knows tons of sad songs," said Carla.

"But we need to find out about Viking *sea* burials," said Penny pointedly.

"It says after the fire they went up to the headland and built him a mound, and offered lots of treasure, and said fine things," said Woody, ignoring her. "Mum and Dad could be involved if we did something like that, because in a way it's a shame. . ." He avoided Carla's eye and his voice trailed off.

"If they're speaking to us afterwards," said Penny. She hugged herself. "I hope Mum doesn't hate us after this."

Carla smoothed back her duvet. "She's never going to find out. I've worked out a way to substitute the coffins, you see; they're all the same. We just need to. . ." She was interrupted by her mother singing loudly downstairs as she cooked dinner.

"O what happened to my true love?
He turned and sailed away
Over the briny ocean
But sent back his ghost to stay. . ."

"She hasn't sung since Grandpa died," said Woody.

"And is that a bad thing?" muttered Penny. "She has to be the only person who listens to *folk* music, on what she refers to as a *ghetto blaster*, on *cassette.*"

"Dad's bringing Gus round tonight, for supper," said Woody. "There's a chance they might go to the barn to see how we're doing."

Carla stared at him. "You could try and get some information out of Gus about his friend Rowan who works at Mr Salt's."

Woody leaned back against the window. Carla wished he wouldn't do that. She was worried he might fall out.

"You don't suppose Gus might want to be a part of it?" Woody ventured.

"A part of what?" snapped Carla, though she knew exactly what he meant.

"He might be useful." Woody was purposefully avoiding her eye.

"You're crazy," said Penny. "Gus – *useful*? He'd shop us straight away. He hates us."

"Yes, but he doesn't hate Grandpa," said Woody. "Dad said they used to spend lots of time together."

"Then we came along and spoiled everything," put in Penny.

"But Gus isn't Grandpa's grandson," said Carla. "He isn't BLOOD."

Woody pulled a face. "So what?"

"If you say anything about this to Gus, I'll . . . I'll . . . I don't know what I'll do but you know it will be VERY BAD," Carla snarled. She didn't like threatening Woody, but this was serious.

"You can be vile sometimes," muttered Woody.

"And you're DERANGED," snapped Carla. "Gus is BAD NEWS. He CAN'T have anything to do with this."

Things got out of hand with everyone roaring at each other until Mum burst in.

"STOP IT!" she yelled. She looked at each of them in turn. She started to tell them off, but changed her mind. "Dinner's ready," she said quietly. "And, Woody Christopher Moon, you'd better eat some of it or I swear I'll go to your school wearing my swimming costume next week."

Penny sniggered.

"I'll even wear my swimming hat," added Mum. "So there."

"But it's November," said Woody. "You'll get cold. You might get ill."

"Then you'd better eat up," said Mum darkly, "or everyone will see me in my bathers. Oh dear, and I need a new swimsuit as mine has a hole in the bottom. Never mind." All three children giggled. "That's better," said Mum. "I don't want you fighting at the moment. We need to love each other, OK? I know it's hard, I know we're all sad, but we've got to stick together. The only thing that is going to make us feel better is each other and time."

"Miss Hame says the only thing that heals the pain of death is a new life," announced Penny.

"Does she?" Mum looked alarmed. "We won't be trying that, I can assure you." She smiled at them. "So come and eat your dinner, which I have lovingly cooked for you." She had cooked a meat pie. Mum must be feeling better, thought Carla. Maybe it was because she'd seen Grandpa. The pie tasted delicious and the pastry melted in their mouths. Even Woody managed a whole portion, and the others had seconds. Mum was beaming at Woody when the phone rang.

"GO AWAY," screamed Mum. She rushed out into the hall, yanked the phone out of the socket, charged back into the kitchen and flung open the window.

"Mum. . ." began Penny.

"GOODBYE," yelled Mum. The children watched as

the telephone flew out of the window. It landed on the path with a clatter. Mum breathed out and turned to face them. "There," she said in a breathless voice. "Now we can eat our dinner in peace." Carla giggled. She was fed up of the phone conversations with sad friends and relations who all said how sorry they were. Why were they sorry? It wasn't their fault Grandpa had died.

"This must be the first full meal you've eaten for days, Woody," said Mum, smiling and sitting back down. Carla nodded at him. It was time to press his advantage.

"Mum" – Woody took the hint – "can we use *Valkyrie* for our entry in the carnival?"

Mum gave him one of her famous looks. "But Grandpa never finished it."

"It's for our *To Valhalla!* entry," said Woody. He glanced at Carla. She was willing him not to mess this up.

"Please, Mum," said Woody, putting down his knife and fork on his empty plate. "Grandpa would have liked it. You know how he was into Vikings, and *Valkyrie* was his best thing, I think. I reckon he'd have loved the idea of it being part of the carnival."

"Yes," said Mum, miles away. "Maybe he would." She looked at them all. "But the boat wasn't his best thing – all of you were." She smiled. "He thought you children were the best ever. He told me."

"Even Gus?" said Woody, avoiding looking at the girls.

"Even Gus," said Mum.

Woody caught Carla's eye.

"All right," said Mum. "But you have to take good care of *Valkyrie*." She looked at Carla. "You're the Carnival Princess. How are you going to be on the royal float AND on the Sparks' one?"

"Carnival people don't call them floats," said Penny. "They call them carts."

"Dad says I ought to be on the royal cart," said Carla, shooting her sister a look. This was no time to be pernickety. "But I can still be involved in *To Valhalla!*" Carla had a secret plan, but before she knew it would work, she had to talk to Sophie. But she hadn't heard from her since Grandpa had died. Carla would worry about that tomorrow. Right now there was an important job to do.

Dummy Run

The telephone rang as soon as Mum plugged it back in. Penny said she was tired and wanted to read so Carla and Woody went out to the garage without her. They attached their small cart to Carla's bike and started collecting things: three boxes of firelighters, matches and small pieces of wood from the log basket. They lifted down the tiny child's-sized wooden rowing boat that Dad kept up in the rafters. They'd not used it for years.

"What are you doing?" asked Penny, appearing in the doorway.

"Dummy run," said Carla. "High tide is at seven-thirty. Woody's coming with me. You stay here and cover for us."

"But it's dark," protested Penny.

"It will be even darker on Friday," said Carla. "I think this operation will only take forty minutes. I have to test the current."

"I'm coming too," said Penny stoutly. "You're not leaving me out."

"But, Penny, it might be dangerous, and you're tired."

"I'm going to be there on the night, so I need to go now," Penny insisted.

"All right," said Carla, looking at her watch. There was no time to argue. "Just stick close to me."

Mum was still on the phone. "It's Maria," she mouthed.

Good, thought Carla, that meant she'd be tied up for ages with baby talk. "Just off to the barn," Carla said. They fled before their mother could object.

The wind was blowing hard. The path was bumpy and the Dugg ran deep and fast below them. The children had lights on their bikes, but it was still hard to see. A big moon occasionally poked out from behind a cloud, but it didn't seem to help much. The children stopped at Grandpa's gate, and Woody ran in to see how the Sparks were getting on.

"There's only Ern and Isla left," he panted when he returned. "I think they fancy each other."

"Don't be stupid," said Carla. They pedalled off into the darkness, the river gurgling below. "Don't go so near the edge," Carla shouted as Woody wobbled close to the slope.

"You'll make me fall off by shouting at me," yelled back Woody.

Penny was quiet as she doggedly pedalled along. Carla wondered if she should have insisted her sister stayed behind, but it was impossible to force Penny to do anything. They stopped at a gate and Woody and Carla lifted the cart through. They looked down the slope to the silvery-black water. Here the Dugg joined the River Wich. And now, just before high tide, the water swirled and pooled, slapping against the muddy banks as the salt water of the big river mingled with fresh water from the Dugg. The children crossed a field and squelched through cowpats and wet grass. Then they joined a rough farm track. By Carla's calculations, the tide should still be coming in. High tide was at seven-thirty, and by Friday it would be at midnight, leaving them enough time for the carnival and for Carla to sneak off and collect Grandpa, load him into the boat and get back to the beach as the tide turned. After high tide, there was slack water for about twenty minutes; then the water swept back out to sea at an astonishing rate. Carla was counting on a strong tide to sweep Grandpa out to sea. The last thing she wanted was to set the boat alight and then have it bob around near the shore. She wanted it out and deep as quickly as possible.

It was getting darker every minute as they moved further and further away from the lights of Little Wichley and the far-off orange glow of Bigwich. And now there was a rushing, pounding sound, growing louder all the time. It was the sound of the sea.

"Grandpa would have loved this!" called Woody.

"He'd have said we were crazy," said Penny.

"Shh," said Carla. The farm track finished at a narrow public road. Just opposite they could see the lights of a cottage.

"Turn off your lights," said Carla in a hushed voice. "The last thing we want to do is draw attention to ourselves."

The children cycled in the darkness along the road through the tiny settlement at Gundy Head. There were a couple of farms and a few houses. The lights from an industrial chicken shed helped them to see where they were going. But soon they had broken away from the houses and were whizzing through the darkness along the coast road. The lights of Sinkworthy nuclear power station twinkled in the distance.

"Is it true that the water is warmer in the sea around the power station?" called out Woody.

"Yes," called Carla. She was less worried about noise now they were away from civilization. "Dad says they pump water around the engines to cool them, then pump it back into the sea."

"Perfect for a swim," observed Penny, whizzing past. They pedalled into the tiny car park by the shore. There wasn't much here, just a battered notice.

GUNDY HEAD
DANGER – DEEP MUD
STRONG OFFSHORE CURRENTS

Another board pictured some faded seabirds. A broken metal fence was half-buried in the dunes. The place was deserted. The wind was blowing harder now, and Carla felt her fingers going numb with cold. They leaned their bikes up against the sand dunes and unhooked the cart.

"Come on," said Carla. "Let's get this over with." They slid over the dunes and on to the beach, bumping the cart over the sand and shingle. They passed a derelict concrete structure consisting of a low platform overlooking the sea supported by four short, fat pillars. Crumbling steps led to the top. Carla thought it was a relic left over from the last war. A few minutes later, just at the high tide line, they reached old Barney's mud horses, nestled in amongst a line of seaweed. These were wooden structures, like a bench on skis, which were weighted with chains against the tide. Barney, a friend of Grandpa's, used them for fishing way out on the flats. It meant he could skate across the mud, carrying his equipment without risk of sinking. The water wasn't yet at high tide. There was an expanse of mud between the children and the waves rolling inland. Carla frowned and hugged herself against the cold. It should be high tide NOW. She took a step forward and the mud sucked at her boots. She knew the mud was firm for a little way. They'd walked on it lots of times, but never in the dark. Every instinct told her not to venture out on the mudflats when the tide was coming in.

"I'm going out there," said Carla. If the ground got too sticky, she'd just turn round and come back.

"I'll come too," said Penny.

"NO," said Woody. "This is stupid. The tide is still coming in. If you put the boat on the water, it's just going to end up on the shore again."

"Then we need to wait," said Carla. "Someone should go back to the barn and borrow Ern's mobile phone to ring Mum and say we're going to be late. It had better be you, Woody, because Penny shouldn't go alone."

"I don't mind," said Penny.

"Forget it," said Carla.

The children stood arguing about who was going to do what when Woody suddenly shouted, "Look!"

The water was just yards away. The children stepped back off the mud and on to the shingle. "That was quick," Carla said slowly.

"How do we know when it's high tide?" asked Penny nervously.

"By looking at your watch," said Carla. "Penny, you have to wait at the top of the sand dunes."

"No," said Penny.

Carla sighed. "If you go and wait at the top of that sand dune, I'll give you two pounds when we get home," she said.

"Three," said Penny.

"Two-fifty," said Carla.

"Done." Penny crossed the sand and scrambled up the dune.

The water rolled nearer, each wave coming closer and closer up the mud. As the children watched, the water seemed to slow. Then there was a sort of lull when the moon came out from behind a cloud. Everything seemed to go quiet.

"I think this is slack water," said Carla looking at her watch. "We've got maybe twenty minutes before it starts pulling out." She set about getting things ready, taking the little wooden boat from the cart and filling it with firelighters. Then she waited. They watched the lights of a faraway aeroplane blink across the sky.

"Let's do it," said Carla. She felt unable to wait a minute longer. She stepped into the shallows and felt the cold water through her wellies. She gently set the boat in the sea and, as Woody held it steady, soaked it with a can of paraffin stolen from the garage.

"I wonder what the dolphins are going to say about that," remarked Penny from the top of the sand dune. "I thought you were a member of the Green Action Group for Cleaner Seas. They'd sack you after this." She shone her torch directly into Carla's face. "Hypocrite."

"Oh, shut up," said Carla. She had spilled a little of the paraffin on her skin and it stank, even after she rinsed her hands in the freezing waves. Then she looked at Woody and they took a few tentative steps deeper into the water, their feet sinking into the mud.

"Deeper," said Carla. "If we let her go here, she'll just wash up on the shore." The beach sloped gently and they had waded out a fair way before the water was sloshing around the tops of their boots.

"No further," said Woody, and Carla squealed as chilling seawater poured into her wellies and she felt herself sinking into the mud.

"Matches," she gasped to Woody. There was a silence. All that could be heard was the lapping waves and the wind whistling through the dunes and seagrass. "I can't find them," said Woody in a small voice.

"WHAT?" shouted Carla. Why did she have to do everything round here? "You idiot." Woody shrank away from her and let go of the boat. It bobbed off a little way so Carla had to splash in the water to get it before it was swept away. "Woody!" she yelled. She was wet up to her knees and the mud was pulling at her.

"Oh, here they are, in a different pocket." He held out the matches.

Carla took them and looked at Woody, shivering in the wobbly torchlight, the water sloshing around his knees. "Sorry I shouted," she said as she pushed the boat back to Woody and struck a match. It promptly blew out. So did the second one, and the third. Gritting her teeth, Carla carefully cupped her hand and struck a fourth match. Sheltering the flame, she lowered it to the wood. She let go and drew her hand back as the paraffin caught fire with a whoosh.

"Get back," shse said to Woody as the wood burned. They splashed towards the shore, but Carla stumbled as she felt the ground give way beneath her. "Woody!" she screamed as the water rose over her hips. "I'm sinking." Woody edged back through the waves and grabbed her hand. With a mighty effort Carla pulled her leg out of the mud. It felt like she was going to pull it right out of its socket. "Woody," whispered Carla. It was a long walk back to dry land. At any step there could be another mud hole. They stood, clutching each other and shivering.

"We'll take it very slowly, single file," said Woody. "I'll go first." Carla nodded, her teeth chattering, and slowly the pair edged their way back to the beach. Penny was waiting for them white-faced at the water's edge.

"What took you so long?" she said. "I couldn't see what you were up to. Why are you so wet?" But Carla only half heard her. Her hand was stinging ferociously, like something was biting her. Instinctively she plunged it into the salt water and howled as the sting grew more intense. She whipped her hand out of the water, but the burning sensation got even worse.

"You must have got burnt," said Woody helpfully. "Is it bad?" Carla could only grunt as she thrust her hand underwater once more. She should have known to drop the match sooner. She should have thought of the danger. The paraffin was bound to catch quickly. She'd seen Dad light fires with paraffin and he always used a taper. But like a fool she had got too close.

"When you said this was a practice run, I didn't think you meant we were actually going to burn somebody," drawled Penny. Carla was furious with herself. She couldn't afford to get injured; there was too little time and too much to do. But secretly she was relieved it was she who had been injured and not one of the others. That would have been awful.

"Are you OK?" Woody touched her back. "Let me see. Penny, shine the torch over here." Carla showed her hand to Woody. In the torchlight they could see a big blister bubbling on her wrist. Carla felt faint and breathless. The pain was incredible. She couldn't think about anything else.

"Hope you don't get infected by all the sewage," said Penny helpfully. "And think of all the radioactivity in the water from the power station."

"THERE IS NO RADIOACTIVITY IN THE WATER. SHUT UP, PENNY," yelled Woody.

"Look—" began Penny, but Woody interrupted her.

"Penny. . ."

"No, look."

The children looked around for the boat, but it had gone. Or the flames had gone out, Carla supposed.

"It's out there. . ." Penny pointed. The boat had been swept some distance away, too far to retrieve it. The flames were tall and danced and flickered in the dark night, reflecting golden patterns on the water. It was getting smaller every second. They watched as it bobbed and swirled. Carla straightened up. "It's working," she said. The wind flattened the flames at intervals and they licked out over the sea, and golden sparks shot into the air. Minutes passed as they watched the fire dance on the water.

"But how do we get Grandpa out there without drowning in the mud?" asked Woody. "There's a strong offshore wind tonight, which would have helped drive it out. But who knows what wind we'll have on Friday." He stood watching the boat burn. "We'll need to use the sails, but we'll have to tie the tiller midships and fit the daggerboard so she doesn't capsize. That will mean putting it in place once we've waded out deep enough."

"What's he on about?" asked Penny.

Nobody answered. The sky had started to rumble and growl. The children fell to their knees. Then a powerful beam of light swept over the water just where the little boat burned.

"Turn off the torch," screamed Carla as a monstrous helicopter burst out of the sky.

The Hunt

"**R**UN!" yelled Carla, grabbing Woody by the collar and dragging him and the cart over the sand. The searchlights of the helicopter swept along the shore, just where they'd been standing.

"To the war platform," panted Carla as the roaring grew deafening. She ducked under the concrete and Woody dived after her. They wrenched Penny underneath as the powerful beams trained overhead. The children huddled in the darkest corner as the lights probed their feet.

"What's happening?" whispered Penny. "Are we being bombed?"

"No," said Carla grimly. "We're being hunted." It hadn't occurred to her that the fire might be seen as dangerous. But the burning boat was bobbing around close to the nuclear plant. Sinkworthy power station was a normal part of their landscape. It was just a series of grey boxes on the horizon where Dad went to work.

"Oh dear," said Woody. Carla saw that he was thinking the same as her. After all the trouble in London on the tubes, when bombs had gone off, everyone had become worried about Sinkworthy being a target for terrorists.

"We need to get out of here," shouted Carla. The air around them was filled with noise and seemed to vibrate.

"Oh God, is it going to land?" Woody whimpered. The searchlights swept up and down the beach.

"They'll see the bikes," shouted Penny, wide-eyed with alarm.

Carla watched the boat still burning bright on the water.

"Oh no," said Woody. A winking red eye was racing through the sky, a second helicopter. The power station, unusually, looked as brightly lit as a Christmas tree as the second helicopter flew right over it and hovered above the flaming boat.

"When I say 'Go', we move it, OK?" Carla took Penny's hand. The chopper circling the boat now started back to shore.

"Go!" screamed Carla, and ran. Woody was with her, but Penny hadn't moved.

"My legs have gone to sleep," she moaned. "I can't go anywhere."

"MOVE," yelled Carla in a growling voice which

shocked even her. It came from her very depths. She sounded like a demon-witch. She hauled Penny out from under the platform and propelled her along the sand and up the dunes until they slithered down into the car park. Blue flashing lights were appearing in the distance. For a moment Carla froze. Then she saw Woody pedalling fast out of the car park. The whole sky was lit up with lights from the choppers and the police cars and the power station.

"Come on," shouted Woody. Carla looked down at Penny, a blue light playing over her stricken face.

"*When you get in a tight fix,*" said Grandpa, "*the best thing is to fix it.*"

An image of Grandpa's face came into her mind. He was smiling and scratching his beard.

"*Go on, lucky legs.*" He nodded. "*Take the footpath over the fields. They won't be looking there. You've got a chance. Take it.*"

All at once Carla was moving again. She knew what to do now. She hefted Penny on to her bike and gave her a shove. "The footpath," she yelled. They raced down the road, the wind whistling in their ears. The choppers were going back and forth over the beach, then back to the little boat. Carla gasped. Black dots dangling from one of the choppers now hovering over the shore. They were lowering men down on to the beach!

"Car coming," bellowed Woody up ahead. "Get in the ditch." He got off his bike and threw it in the deep ditch that ran by the side of the road. Penny and Carla copied and they all crouched low in the wet. A police car, blue lights flashing and siren wailing, flew past. Carla counted to ten, listening. There were more sirens, but they sounded further away. "Go," she shouted. The gate to the fields was just around the next bend. They dragged their bikes and the cart out of the ditch and back to the road. In seconds all three were speeding to the gate. Carla wondered if they were going to make it before another police car came by. The gate was shut. Carla shoved Woody out of the way when he fumbled with the catch, but she couldn't open it either.

"Chuck the bikes over," she ordered. One by one the children heaved the bikes over. They made nasty clanking sounds as they landed.

"My bike," complained Penny.

"Come *on*," said Carla, practically throwing her sister over. She pulled herself over the gate, banging her shin on the metal bars and falling to the ground on the other side. All three children scrambled into the shadow of the hedge as another police car rushed by. As soon as the lights had faded they got on their bikes and pedalled down the bumpy footpath over the field.

"If a helicopter goes over he'll see us – there's no cover," panted Woody.

"We'd have to hide in the rhyne," said Carla, her heart thumping. "Now move." The path was dimly visible cutting through the centre of a flat ploughed field. It ran right alongside a broad rhyne. The water was dark and still. Carla glanced back to see if anyone was following them and her bike lurched on a stone. Only by throwing her weight in the other direction did she prevent herself from toppling into the water.

"Listen." Woody stopped as a new siren joined the cacophony. "I'd swear that's a fire engine." The children watched as halfway up the hill to the right of them a flashing vehicle sped along the main road, then turned on to the coast road.

"It was only a little fire," muttered Carla. The children bumped and bounced over the plough ruts. The farmer had ploughed through the footpath so they had no choice but to cycle in the furrow, having to navigate big, hard clods of earth. It wasn't easy, especially for Carla, who was towing the cart. The wheels kept getting snarled up on stones and earth and weeds.

A helicopter buzzed up in front of them, and Woody shrieked and overbalanced. He tumbled down the bank and into the rhyne as the chopper roared over their heads, heading straight for the sea. Woody had gone right underwater, but his head broke the surface only seconds later. "C-c-cold," he coughed, and struggled to the bank, covered in mud. Carla rushed to help. She looked back at Penny. "You keep going. I'll get him out." She grabbed her brother's sopping wet sleeve and hauled him up the bank.

"Watch out for leeches," called Penny as she pedalled off.

Woody sat panting on the ground. "It's freezing," he

gasped, sounding surprised. He shook his head and drops of water hit Carla in the face. They watched as Penny reached the far hedge. She lifted her bike through the stile and melted into the darkness.

"She'll be OK now. It's only two minutes to Grandpa's," said Carla. "Are you ready to go?"

"Look," squeaked Woody as the chopper hurtled out of the sky towards them.

"Down!" shouted Carla as blinding beams of lights swung slowly over the field and along the rhyne. The children pressed themselves into the ground but the light was getting closer, closer.

"Look at that," said Woody with terrified fascination as a dark figure climbed the far style and began running at them.

"It's not Penny," said Carla, a new, slow kind of terror rising up in her. Even in the darkness she could see this running shadow was big. As big as a full-grown man. "Oh, Penny," Carla whispered. She should never, never have let her sister go off on her own. The searchlights were coming back and the figure was running hard towards them. Carla held her breath. There could be no escape.

He was about six feet tall, with a shock of black hair and a pale angry face. He was dressed all in black. Carla felt a wave of horror, coupled with a strange kind of relief. It was all over now.

"Get over to that bush," barked the man, pointing. "Sinkworthy's on red alert." He picked up the bikes and dumped them in the water. Then he ran to a low thorn bush and wriggled under. Carla and Woody gave each other a terrified look and flew after him. "Come on – it's hollow under here," he said. "Hurry up, nitwits."

They all lay breathing heavily as the helicopter chocked overhead.

"Did you see Penny?" whispered Carla.

"I sent her back to the barn. Honestly, what are you kids up to?"

"Please don't tell on us," pleaded Carla. "Please, Gus."

Gus

They lay in the cold damp hollow beneath the thorn bush as the air thundered around them. "You've really done it this time," shouted Gus over the noise. "Who do you think you are? The Famous Five?"

"Oh, shut up," muttered Carla. She'd forgotten that he was coming to supper tonight.

"Carla, you've got a serious attitude problem," shouted Gus.

"What are you doing following us around, anyway?" snapped Carla. Her wrist was stinging. Beside her Woody was shaking uncontrollably. And where was Penny?

"There's gratitude for you," yelled Gus. "I've just saved you from the SAS!"

"How did you find us?"

"Dad's having his tea so Freya sent me out," said Gus, lowering his voice as the noise subsided. The chopper had moved to the far end of the field. "It's dark, it's eight o'clock. She said I'd find you in the barn."

Carla grimaced; she hadn't realized it was that late already. Oh wow, they were going to be in trouble – especially her.

"I found a snotty kid defacing Grandpa's boat and no sign of you three nut-buckets anywhere. The kid wouldn't tell me where you were, so that made me think you were up to something," said Gus. "I did a little guesswork."

"How did you work it out?" asked Carla, her heart sinking. Did Gus suspect anything?

"There aren't many places to go around here," said Gus. "I'd already checked the bird hide. And anyway, if it wasn't for me, you'd be in an army cell by now. I saw the burning from the road. Are you totally dumb? How could you think you could send a burning object out to sea yards from the power station without causing a national security scare? Have you got no idea about the political climate?"

"Excuse me," interrupted Woody, "I'm dying of hypothermia here. Can we make a run for it?" The night had plunged back into darkness as the third chopper had joined the others at the shore. Gus wriggled out of the bush a little way.

"Right, infants," he emphasized the word. "When I say 'Now', you need to make for the stile. Then run fast along the river path. Keep close to the hedge. Get to the barn as quick as you can. If you see anybody

101

coming, lie down. If you are by the ditch, jump in it. OK?"

"OK," said Carla. She would never usually take orders from Gus, but on this occasion he seemed to have some good ideas. Her heart was still hammering in her chest.

There was a pause.

"Go," Gus whispered. Carla pulled herself out of the hollow, but a twig caught her hair and she yelped as her head was yanked back.

"I'll do it," said Woody, unhooking her.

"Come on, rats," said Gus, who was already out of the bush and running. Carla crawled out of the bush, got to her feet. She looked round for Woody, who was next to her. She nodded at him, and then they ran. Carla didn't think she had ever run as fast. Once she landed awkwardly and her ankle went all tingly, but she told herself it wasn't too bad and pounded on. They reached the gate in no time and Gus vaulted over and dragged them after him. Carla had never seen him so active. Now they were pelting down the gravel path by the river towards the lights of Little Wichley. Gus had hold of Woody's arm, pulling him along. In minutes they were at Grandpa's gate, breathing heavily.

"In," ordered Gus, pulling aside the metal sheeting and shoving Carla hard in the back. They stumbled up the path through the dark garden and fell into the barn. Carla blinked in the sudden light. She sank gratefully on to a wooden chair, noticing Woody panting on the ground next to her, and Penny talking to Ern by the tyre mountain.

"What have you been up to?" asked Ern, bemused. "Your scary brother has been round terrorizing us. And it sounds like a war zone out there. We've had helicopters flying really low for the last twenty minutes."

"Gus isn't my brother," said Carla. She bit her lip as Gus walked through the door, putting his mobile phone into his pocket. She wondered if he'd heard.

They all froze as a helicopter thundered overhead. It stayed for a minute, then roared away.

"Freya and Dad are on their way," said Gus. "I've just rung them." He grinned. "You are in trouble."

"You couldn't. . . You didn't. . ."

"Yep," said Gus. "I told them everything. They know you set fire to something and sent it out to sea."

"What was the point of hiding us," said Woody, "when you've gone and told on us anyway?" He shrugged off his wet coat and jumper and looked round for something to put on. Carla went behind the tyre mountain and fetched him Grandpa's blanket.

Gus snorted. "I saved you from the SAS, but I can't save you from Dad."

"But who is it out there?" asked Woody. "It can't be the army, not really."

"Yes, it is," said a man's voice as the barn door swung open.

The children froze as the man strode into the barn. He was wearing his slippers.

"Dad," said Penny. She ran to hug him as Mum also appeared. "Woody, why are you so wet? Carla, you're soaked too. What HAVE you been doing?" Mum's face was white and her voice was clipped. This didn't stop her pulling off Woody's wet T-shirt, stripping off her cardigan and wrapping it round him, then ordering him to take off his wet trousers RIGHT NOW. Woody vanished behind the tyre mountain. Then Mum lifted Penny right up, giving her a long hug. When she set her down she reached for Carla. "What have you done to your arm, sweetheart?" Her voice softened. "That looks sore."

"I just burnt it a bit," said Carla. It was really hurting her now. As Mum examined it there was the roar of the chopper. Penny lifted the material that Grandpa had used as a curtain and they watched the bright lights hurtle about the sky. Woody emerged from the tyre mountain wearing Grandpa's blanket as a skirt.

"They've found us," he said hoarsely.

"We should get home," said Dad. "I don't want my family mixed up with Her Majesty's forces."

They waited until the noise had subsided, then Dad ordered everyone outside. Gus was despatched to take Ern home. The children listened to him protesting all the way down the street. "I'm THIRTEEN years old. And it's only eight o'clock. What's your problem?"

"You kids are the problem," they heard Gus growl.

"If we get stopped, we're just on a family walk," said Dad. "Up to see Grandpa's barn. OK?"

"You mean you're not going to tell on us?" whispered Carla.

"No," said Dad. "But once we get inside, you are going to have to tell me exactly what you are up to." The family hurried along the riverbank. The lights of their house were blazing.

"You left the back door open," said Penny. Everyone hurried up through the garden and into the house. Nelson stretched and miaowed in greeting as they trooped in. Carla shut her eyes again. She wasn't going to enjoy the next few hours.

"Let me sort out your wrist," said Mum. She went over to the sink and filled a bowl of water. She brought the bowl over to Carla and plunged her wrist into it. The relief was instant. "Keep it in there," she ordered. "It's a nasty little burn, but you'll be OK. Why are you so filthy?"

"Do you have any idea how worried we were?" interrupted Dad as he examined the mud-stained soles of his slippers. "You were late, and you weren't where you were supposed to be."

Mum lifted her head. "We've just lost Grandpa," she said. "And then ALL of you put me through this. How could you?" Her voice broke.

Dad rubbed his head. "You've caused a major security alert. At the power station we're constantly having meetings and talks about security. We are supposed to be super-vigilant. We're even supposed to check out friends and family and make sure they aren't looking at stuff they shouldn't, and now Gus tells me you three go and burn a toy boat just by the plant. Are you mad?"

"Come on then," said Mum, folding her arms. "What were you doing out there? What can possibly be more important than the Sparks' cart?"

Nobody spoke. Dad sat heavily on the sofa, his gaze never leaving Carla's face. "How could you even risk upsetting your mother at a time like this? I'd have thought better of you all, especially you, Carla. I thought you were SENSIBLE."

"It's not that bad," said Penny. "We only set fire to a toy and sent it out to sea."

"That's not bad, not on its own," admitted Dad. "What is bad is lying to your parents about where you were, and being very late, and scaring us silly, at a time when we are ALL in deep sorrow. It's insensitive. It's crass. . . It's. . ."

"Sorry," whispered Carla. "We didn't mean to upset you." She couldn't believe everything was going so badly.

Dad puffed his cheeks out and sat back in his chair. Nelson jumped on his lap and Carla noted he didn't push her off. She sent a secret eye-meet to the others. If Dad was in a really bad mood, he wouldn't have let Nelson sit on him. Carla pulled her wrist out of the water and examined the burn. Her skin was a bubble of angry red.

"So whatever got into you?" asked Mum, dropping a

large towel on to Carla's lap and giving her a searching look.

There was a decision to be made. Now was the perfect chance to come clean about the whole scheme. If Carla admitted they were doing a test run of an attempt to burn Grandpa's body – after stealing him from the morgue to recreate for him the funeral of a Viking king – then yes, sure there would be some astonishment, some punishment even, but maybe, eventually, some understanding. But the game would be up, and the plan would be over. Grandpa's last request would not be fulfilled, before they'd even properly tried. Something told Carla that Grandpa wouldn't mind if they failed to give him his preferred funeral, as long as they had really tried. But she couldn't give up at the first hurdle. She could just picture him shaking his head.

"There's no such thing as luck," he'd say. *"But hard graft often leads to success."*

She shot a look at the others. Woody was shivering and Penny wouldn't meet her eye. She couldn't just blow it without consulting everyone else. She couldn't give up now. Not yet. She thought of Grandpa, lying in that hideous funeral parlour. She wasn't ready to say goodbye to him that way. She took another long, slow breath.

"Can I just go and change my trousers?" Carla leapt up and grabbed a clean pair from the pile of laundry on the table. She ducked into the hall and peeled off her wet jeans.

She was going to lie.

Carla used to be good at lying. When she was little she lied all the time, so much that the children at school used to sing, "*Liar, liar, pants on fire. . .*"

From an early age she had hoodwinked her parents with all sorts of stuff: until she was eight years old she lied all the time, about her friends, her homework, about whether she had tidied her bedroom or whether she had shared the biscuits with the others. She'd lied about bigger things too, like how the teacher said she was best in the class at maths, and how she'd scored ten out of ten in the spelling test when really she'd only got six. Or that she'd spent her dinner money on just that, dinner, and not stored it all away in her money box to spend on sweets and comics. She didn't know why she did it, but she did know she couldn't stop. Not until the Accident, after which she had sworn never to lie again.

It was the river, of course. Everything big seemed to centre round the river. The main rule was, "No going in *Julie* without an adult." This was an ENORMOUS rule. A rule so mighty even Carla wouldn't have dared to break it. But one evening Woody spilled his drink all over her school bag and her project on Ancient Egypt had been ruined, and she had hit him and he had hit her back. Mum was out in the front garden with Penny, talking to a neighbour, and Woody and Carla ended up having a fight. Not just a play fight, a proper one, with hair pulling, kicking and scratching. Woody had walloped her in the stomach and she'd punched him in the back. They were both crying and shouting. There had never been a fight like this before (or since), and as Carla was bigger she was winning, and Woody finally ran off, with Carla chasing him out of the back door and down the garden. Mum usually kept the river gate bolted and padlocked shut, but for some reason today she had just bolted it and the padlock hung open. Carla fled after Woody as he opened the gate and ran along the riverbank.

"Go away," he had howled. But seeing his weakness had made Carla even madder. Woody scrambled down the bank, on to the little wooden jetty and into *Julie*. "Get back," he had screamed, tears and snot pouring down his face.

It made Carla shiver to remember it.

Looking at him wobbling in that boat had finally made her anger subside, so instead of going after him she turned on her heel and stalked back into the house. Then Mum had come in, with a worried look on her face.

"What was that noise? There was such a racket I couldn't hear Miss Hame. And where's Woody?"

Carla shrugged. "I don't know," she'd said, stalking off. She never knew why she'd said that. If she'd said, "In the boat," Woody would have got into trouble, and surely that was what she was after. But she was fed up with him. She just wanted to be on her own. Besides, *Julie* was moored. Woody wasn't going anywhere. Carla remembered running up to her room and slamming the door. She'd sat seething on the bed and examining the scratches on her arms. Then she'd emptied out her school bag and set about salvaging the contents. She got so absorbed she didn't really take any notice of the noise from downstairs.

"Woody, *Woody*. Where are you, Woody?" Mum was tearing around the house. Penny was calling too. "WOODY, WOODEEEEEE. . ." She was only small but even she sounded worried. The watercolour picture of the Valley of the Kings was ruined. There was no doubt about it. Carla wished she'd thumped Woody even harder. There was a crash outside in the garden beneath her window.

"Ouch." Mum hopped up and down. She'd knocked into the log pile. "CARLA," she bellowed, "WHERE IS YOUR BROTHER?"

Carla stared out of the window and watched her mother as she looked down the garden. When Mum saw the garden gate was unlatched, she froze.

"WOODY!" Mum screamed and pelted down the garden towards the river, dragging Penny after her. Carla's stomach turned over. She shouldn't have left him in the boat on his own. She dropped her painting and flew down the stairs. In seconds Carla was at the river. The first thing she noticed was that *Julie* was bobbing *upside down*. Her line was snarled up in some brambles trailing in the far side of the river.

"*Woody?*" whispered Carla. Those few seconds were the most terrifying of her life. But suddenly there he was, struggling up the bank, like some kind of river animal covered in mud. He kept slipping back into the water. The mud was too deep for him to get out and the little jetty was too far upstream for him to reach. Mum shoved Penny at Carla and ran over towards Woody. She slid a little way down the bank and reached out to him.

"Come on, darling," she said. "Grab my hand." But Woody couldn't reach; he kept slithering away. Mum whipped off her T-shirt and threw one end to Woody to catch. Now he could reach.

"Hold on tight, sweetheart," said Mum, and she hauled him up the bank. When he reached the top she held him close. Carla remembered seeing her back and bra all covered with mud from Woody. Mum held him tightly for ages and then she burst into tears and cried and cried as if she would never stop.

Later, when everyone was cleaned up, Carla was in the Worst Trouble of Her Life. She still shuddered when she remembered that afternoon. After her mother had dealt with her, Carla was sent to her room for the rest of the afternoon. It felt like for ever. Carla had lain on her bed weeping, convinced that her mother didn't love her any more. Even Dad, usually on her side, had stormed at her when he'd come home.

The next day she had gone to see Grandpa and had told him everything. "She hates me," she'd said miserably as Grandpa had fixed her a mug of coffee.

"*It's as much of a lesson for her as it is for you,*" said

Grandpa. "*That gate should have been locked. And she doesn't hate you; she loves you, very much.*"

A week or so after the accident, when everyone had calmed down, Mum and Carla had made a pact.

"I'll try not to make you look after the others too much, if you'll agree not to lie to me," said Mum. And Carla had agreed. It would be nice not to have to always feel responsible for the little ones, especially when she was quite little herself. It was an event which changed her, and Mum, and even Woody, because he worked harder at his swimming after that, to get his blue badge.

"*A sailor has to know how to swim,*" said Grandpa.

And after that, Carla had never told another lie – hardly. Well, not to her parents anyway. And now, after years, she was about to break that promise. She came back into the kitchen and looked her mother in the eyes. "I burned myself with a match," she said. "We were just messing around by the beach. We burned the toy boat."

Mum looked at her long and hard. "I've worked that out already," she said. "Kit, could you get those two into the bath and then into bed?" Carla looked at the floor. She wanted to go to bed too. As Dad herded the others up the stairs Woody shrugged as if to say, "It's up to you."

"Come on then, why were you burning. . .?"

There was a loud *thump, thump* on the front door. Through the curtains they could see a flickering blue light in the road.

"Up to bed," whispered Mum. "Now! Get into your pyjamas; tell the others to do the same."

"But, Mum—"

"No," muttered Mum. "On second thoughts, wash your face, brush your hair and put on this." She dived behind the chair and brought out a large cardboard box. "Mrs Roach brought it round." There was another thump on the door. Mum ripped open the box and pulled out a vast pink shimmery dress. "Go, go, go." She pulled Carla to her feet and propelled her to the stairs, thrusting the dress in her arms. "You've been with the Sparks and you came home an hour ago," she said.

"IS ANYONE IN?" said a loud and annoyed male voice, and Carla fled.

"Go." Mum shoved Woody's wet clothes behind the sofa and emptied the bowl of water into the sink. Upstairs the others were already in their pyjamas and Dad was supervising the face washing. Everyone stared at the dress.

"Good evening. Police. Can we have a word?" They heard the voice booming up the stairs.

"Good idea," whispered Dad, looking at the dress. "Get into it, quickly. I'll go down. Remember, none of you were at the beach. It wouldn't be good for me at work if this came out. And your mother is under too much stress as it is."

Carla crept over the landing into her bedroom. She pulled off her dirty clothes and kicked them under the bed. She worked out which was the front of the pink concoction and slipped it over her head. It was her Carnival Princess dress and was awful. It was like the sort of thing she'd seen crazy mothers on the telly dress their tiny tots in, to compete in teeny beauty pageants. The material smelled plasticky and it scratched her neck. She couldn't wear this in front of everyone. But the dress fitted. The skirt flounced out from her waist and dipped to the floor. Instead of making her look like a three-year-old, it made her look older. And the colour seemed to make her eyes flash. She must need her head examined. She was wearing a pink ball dress. She, Carla Moon, did not wear pink dresses. She tutted and was about to take the horrible thing off when she heard her mother calling her.

"Carla, this gentleman would like a word with you. Can you come down?" Carla dragged her brush through her hair and pulled off her dirty wet socks. She was going to have to lie again. But this time Mum actually *wanted* her to. She grabbed a silk scarf and loosely draped it over her sore arm. She turned the handle of her bedroom door.

There was only one policeman downstairs. He was slightly overweight with a red face and he sat on the very edge of the sofa. There was hardly any of his bottom on the seat. Carla wondered how he didn't fall off. He didn't seem to notice her when she came down; he was so busy talking to Dad. Mum was the closest to him, but he addressed all his words to Dad, like Mum wasn't even there. She wouldn't like that. Mum didn't like being ignored. She liked being the centre of everything.

"So we suspect it's just kids, but you can understand, in the current political climate, events like this are taken extremely seriously and. . ."

He caught sight of Carla and stopped talking.

"You look nice," said Dad, winking at her. "I never thought I'd see you in pink, though," he added.

"My daughter is this year's Bigwich Carnival Princess," said Mum, and Carla detected a distinctly boastful tone in her voice.

"She looks bonnie," said the policeman. "They made the right choice."

Carla gave him her sweetest smile.

"This your eldest?" huffed the police officer. "She doesn't look like she's been committing acts of arson with cans of paraffin on a dark muddy beach."

"Pardon?" said Carla delicately, noticing her parents bristle at the mention of paraffin.

"If you hear anything, let us know. We'd like to confirm which kids did it." He rose from the chair.

When the policeman had gone, there was a long, long silence.

Mum was the first to break ranks; she crossed the room to the curtains and peeped through a crack. "He's gone next door." She folded her arms and looked at Carla.

"Now what was that about paraffin?"

Betrayal

"So that's it," whispered Penny later that night. The children were holding an emergency meeting in her bedroom long after their parents were asleep. "Grandpa is going to end up stuck next to Grandma."

Mum and Dad seemed to believe that they were just playing on the beach. They hadn't connected the fire with Grandpa's death. Apart from a long lecture about arson and not using paraffin, Carla thought they had sort of got away with it.

Woody sat cross-legged at the end of the bed, looking out of the window. The police and helicopters had gone away hours ago. The only sounds were the river rushing out to sea and the whisper of the wind. "I don't remember much about Grandma," he said to no one in particular. "But I have one memory. I was watching Carla dance in a garden somewhere. There were lots of people. Maybe it was a wedding. I don't

116

know. And all I can remember is a horrible old woman in a red flowery dress yanking my thumb out of my mouth over and over again."

"That was Grandma," said Carla. "It was at Aunty Vi's wedding. Grandma said boys should never suck their thumbs. She kept bugging you until you cried and spoiled the speeches. You were only three. Mum was mad about it."

Woody shook his head sadly. "I can still remember her rings scratching me. And she smelled of poo."

"I think you may have imagined that, Woody," said Carla. "Grandma was always very clean. She told Mum that unless she bathed us every day we'd get infected with some deadly disease."

"So why did Grandpa marry her in the first place?" asked Penny.

Carla thought of the letters she'd found in Napoleon's neck, but said nothing. She wasn't ready to read them yet. She'd hidden them in her room, in amongst her books.

"I'm not giving up," said Woody firmly. "*To Valhalla!* is coming on nicely. We've got our placement changed on the carnival listings. No more *Bananas in Pyjamas*. We've done a test run; the boat burned. It got swept out to sea. We've still got a couple of days to make the rest of the props. We're nearly there, aren't we?"

"No," said Carla, "we are not nearly there." She didn't like to tell them that she hadn't yet worked out how she was going to collect Grandpa without anyone noticing. She had an idea, but that was all. Also, Ern's dad was going to drive the tractor during the carnival, but he was hardly going take them to the sea afterwards with no explanation. Had Ern meant it when he said he'd drive? But how would they get rid of his dad? Carla hoped that the solutions to these problems would magically reveal themselves when the time came. She knew why she worked like this. The task they faced was so huge – so *impossible* – the only way to proceed was to take it step by step. But now they had only three days until carnival. "But we'll keep going," she concluded. "Who's in?"

"I'm not having Grandma nagging Grandpa for all eternity," said Woody. "But I don't know how we'll get Grandpa sent off properly without causing another security alert."

Carla had been thinking about this too. "It's like the boy who cried wolf," she said. "When they see another fire in the sea, they'll think it's the same kids. Maybe they won't respond so dramatically. But it does mean we have to work quickly if we don't want to get caught. It makes the whole thing more scary."

Penny let out a deep sigh. "I'm in," she said. "But I wish my bike hadn't got chucked in the rhyne. And there's another important matter." She looked at Carla. "You owe me two pounds fifty."

*

BIGWICH GAZETTE

Local Police Slammed for "Overreaction"

Bristol and Avon Constabulary and the emergency response team were criticized by locals, as they reacted "in disproportionate scale" to an incident just off the coast of Gundy Head on Tuesday night. Three helicopters, four police cars and three fire engines arrived at the scene when a security guard at the nearby Sinkworthy power station alerted the authorities to the presence of a burning object floating just west of its northern coastal boundary. Three army Hawk helicopters searched the coastline for three hours and a door-to-door search was made in the surrounding villages. "It was like living in LA," said Margery Hame, a long-standing resident of Little Wichley and chair of the local WI. "Police were knocking on everyone's doors and the helicopters ruined the peace of the evening. Everyone thought there must be a murderer on the loose." Local sources have revealed that the "burning missile" was a child's boat. Matches were also found on the beach, as well as children's footprints and a small sock.

"We live in testing times," said Chief Superintendent Frank Dopple. "Any threatening behaviour, especially a stone's throw from one of our nuclear power stations, will be taken seriously." However, he later conceded that the boat sank within half an hour and that the fire was most likely the work of children. "We are interviewing local parents as to the whereabouts of their children on Tuesday night. If anyone has any information, we would ask them to come forward, as we would like to clear this matter up. Also, we must stress that it is illegal to light fires on the beaches, and the sea currents, as any local will know, are extremely fierce."

Carla read Wednesday's paper over her father's shoulder.

"Don't do it again," said Dad. "I must have been crazy to cover for you." He sighed. "But you'll get punishment enough on Friday night when you have to wear that awful dress."

"I thought you said you liked it."

Dad didn't reply.

But Carla smiled to herself. It must be good that the authorities had been criticized about last night. Maybe on Friday they wouldn't be quite so quick to react when there was a report of another fire in exactly the same place.

Maybe.

The first task after breakfast was to fish the bikes out of the rhyne. They were slimy with mud, and weeds were wrapped round the spokes. Water gushed from Penny's saddle. The children had to tie a rope round the handlebars of Woody's bike to pull it out. It was so dirty even Woody didn't think he could ride it home. Now the bikes sat in a corner of the barn, the mud drying off them in flakes. Woody had rubbed the worst off with a damp cloth but they were still filthy. Carla left the cart in Grandpa's garden behind a holly bush. She'd deal with it later.

The Sparks were hard at work. *Valkyrie* already looked different. Isla had brought in a collection of oars – goodness knows where she'd got them – and she'd made a cardboard prototype dragon figurehead. Now she was slapping papier mâché on the chicken-wire frame. Samantha and Bullet were designing the costumes. They'd decided that the oarsmen would wear hessian sacks and brown trousers, and anyone who wanted to be a god would have to come up with their own outfit. Woody consulted his photograph. They were referring to the ancient Norwegian Viking ship, the Oseberg ship, which Isla had already mentioned. The ship was found buried in a mound, was over a thousand years old and contained the grave of a queen. It also contained horses, food, clothing, weapons, a cart and even a slave girl. It was a beautiful ship, with ornate carvings and a fantastic curved prow. *Valkyrie*, of course, would look very different, but Woody hoped some of the Oseberg magic might rub off. Grandpa deserved no less.

"We need to sort out the lights," said Ern. "As we haven't got much time, I suggest we use the frame we had made for *Bananas in Pyjamas*. Dad says he'll help us with the electrics. And we've got a generator which is good and loud, but small enough to sit on the back of the trailer."

Everyone started arguing about what music they should have. Carla was sure there was a famous classical piece of music called "The Ride of the Valkyries". Grandpa would know. She swallowed a wave of sadness when she remembered he wouldn't be able to tell her. Ern caught her eye and smiled. "All right?" he mouthed.

Carla nodded, feeling a bit bleak. Sophie, her best friend, liked classical music. Maybe she'd know. She would be wondering why Carla hadn't been in touch. She knew, of course, that Grandpa had died, but they were usually on the phone every day, talking about the same stuff they'd talked about in school. They knew exactly what was going on in each other's lives, but for the last few days Carla had been too busy and too sad to call.

Her thoughts were interrupted by Ratsy emptying out a large sack into the middle of the floor. From the squeals of horror from everyone, it was obviously worth a look. Carla wandered over.

"Look at these beauties," said Ratsy, beaming. He held up a yellowing cow horn.

"Urrgh," said Penny, cupping her hands over her mouth. "It's revolting."

"Cool," said Bullet. "They're gross." He sounded delighted.

"You've got quite a collection," said Isla. "What are they for?"

Ratsy looked puzzled. "For *To Valhalla!* of course." Ratsy's dad worked on a big dairy farm, and, Ratsy explained, every so often a batch of bullocks would need their horns removed so they didn't gore each other. At the end of a dehorning session, amongst the stink of burning bone and hair, there would be a pile of stubby, bloody horns. And sometimes some of the bullocks had grown quite large horns. These were the ones that Ratsy wanted.

"They'd get thrown to the dogs if I didn't take 'em," said Ratsy, shaking his head. Everyone was listening intently. It was amazing, reflected Carla, what people got up to in their spare time.

"You may wonder how I got them so clean," Ratsy went on, enjoying the audience. "Inside, the horns are full of blood and tissue and stuff, bits of the cow's head, I suppose." Penny cleared her throat loudly. "It's too nasty to scrape it out by hand, but I have a clever way of doing it," he continued. "You find a big stick. Then you dig a hole in a patch of earth which isn't going to get ploughed up and you bury your horns. Mark the spot with a stick and cover it with heavy stones to stop your dogs digging up your horns and eating them."

Penny grimaced at Carla.

"Three months later, you dig up your horns, and hey ho! Clean as a whistle," said Ratsy proudly. "I haven't even had to *rinse* these. And now I proudly reveal my collection, that I have been collecting for SIX YEARS. I've been burying horns since I was three years old! And now we can use them in our *To Valhalla!* display. We can all have amazing helmets. Look, I've made one already." He delved into his bag and brought out a cardboard painted hat with two knobbly horns poking out. "We'll look REAL," he said happily.

"But can I have them back afterwards?" He sounded anxious. "Only these are my best thing."

"Thank you, Ratsy," said Ern, stepping forward. "They'll make our costumes fantastic." He looked sternly round at everyone. "Won't they." It was not a question.

"Yes, oh yes," muttered everyone. Though Isla had backed away so much she was practically out of the door.

Woody looked stricken. "But the Vikings never had horns in their helmets," he hissed to Carla. "That was an eighteenth-century invention, during an operatic stage show, to make them look more exciting to the audience. We won't be authentic if we wear them."

"Woody," said Carla firmly, "we are riding a carnival cart called *To Valhalla!* We will be surrounded by hundreds of flashing light bulbs and rowing to music. None of this is authentic. It's supposed to be fun."

"I'm not going to wear one," grumbled Woody.

As a few of the Sparks edged forward to examine Ratsy's horns, Ern touched Carla's arm. "There's something I'm worried about," he said. "Can I have a word?" Carla nodded and followed him behind the tyre mountain. "The thing is," he said, settling on a tyre (Carla was glad he didn't sit on Grandpa's couch), "what are people going to say when we haven't got a float for the other towns on their carnival nights? Everyone is going to be all, like, 'Where's *To Valhalla!*?' People are going to put two and two together when a burning Viking ship is discovered in the bay." He looked into her face. "Should we tell the Sparks our real plans? And even if we did, what are our parents going to say when they inevitably find out what we've done?"

Carla felt panicky. "Shh," she whispered. What if anyone had overheard?

"You should tell the Sparks," said Ern. "And after that we need to make another *To Valhalla!* Maybe we could use *Julie.*"

"Keep your voice down," hissed Carla. "I need to think about it."

"You'd better be quick," said Ern. "We're running out of time."

Carla got up and flounced out into the garden. She felt mad with Ern for pressuring her. But she knew he was right. Once *To Valhalla!* had vanished, everyone would know what they'd done. She looked up at the sky. The temperature had dropped and the wind was up. Carla pulled her coat around her and wished she'd worn a hat. It was the sort of wind that went right through you. Thin clouds were scudding across the sky. She kicked at a mess of leaves blowing over the wet grass. Grandpa always swept up the leaves. He pushed them deep into the hedge and said they'd have a bonfire to burn them up. Now they were scattered all over the grass. A chill travelled down Carla's neck and her eyes filled with tears.

Grandpa couldn't be dead, he just couldn't.

"Carla," said Ern, appearing at her shoulder, "let's go back inside."

"All right?" Woody came over and looked worriedly at the two of them.

"Just cold," Carla said with a weak grin. "Just feeling the cold."

Carla was quiet at lunch time. Apart from worrying about Mum, and covering their tracks with the fake coffin, she'd not given a thought to what happened after Friday. Now Ern was forcing the pace. Would it be possible to make another *To Valhalla!* in just three days? She supposed if they saved the wooden waves, the light-frame and the figurehead and maybe even the flags and bunting from *Valkyrie* it might be possible. They'd just have to smarten *Julie* up. But she was an old boat. Her sails had been packed away for years. They might be holey and mouldy. And Grandpa would have to go out to sea in *Valkyrie* with most of the Viking trimmings removed. Did that still count as a Viking funeral? She sighed deeply. Everything was getting so complicated.

A shrill peal interrupted her thoughts. Mum plodded out into the hall to answer the phone, her leek-and-potato soup half eaten in her bowl.

"It's Sophie." Mum put her head round the door. Carla felt a stab of guilt. She left the room and picked up the receiver.

"Hi."

"You never told me," said Sophie.

"Told you what?"

"About the Viking funeral."

Carla gasped. "What?" How did she know?

"Isla Godfrey knew, but I didn't. I'm sorry about your grandpa, but don't you like me any more?"

Isla! How could she possibly know unless . . . Carla held her breath. There had been a major leak.

"Sophie," she began and stopped. Mum was in the kitchen, just the other side of the hall. She would hear everything Carla said. "I should see you," said Carla. "Can I come over? I'd like to explain. I could come over at five?" She heard a deep sigh on the line.

"All right," said Sophie, and put down the phone. Carla caught sight of herself in the hall mirror. She looked peaky and worried. So Sophie and Isla knew; did anyone else? This was awful. Carla didn't know what to do next. Mum popped her head round the door. "Is everything all right? You haven't seen Sophie for ages."

"Everything's fine," said Carla slowly. In a daze she walked past her mother and sat staring at her soup steaming on the table.

"Let's get back to work," said Woody, pushing his soup bowl away.

"Carla's got her Carnival Princess rehearsal at three," said Mum. "So she'll need to be back here by two-thirty at the latest or I'll come and collect her."

Woody looked aghast. "You *can't*. Our entry is top secret."

"Carla had better not be late then," said Mum grimly.

Everyone except Bullet – whose mum always dropped him off – was already back from lunch. Penny took up her brush to paint the wooden waves which were going to be fixed to each side of the trailer. Woody commenced cutting out fabric triangles for bunting. Once they were settled, Carla cornered Ern and quietly drew him behind the tyre mountain. When she was sure no one was listening, she demanded how Isla and therefore Sophie had found out about the funeral.

"Oh, does Sophie know?" said Ern. "That shouldn't be a problem, should it? Isn't she your best friend?"

"But what about Isla?" said Carla, forgetting to lower her voice. "How on earth does she know?"

Ern looked her in the eye. "I told her on Monday," he said quietly. "At the same time I told everyone else."

"YOU WHAT?" shrieked Carla.

"They had to know," said Ern. "You can't do it without us, can you? And you can trust us."

"How dare you?" Carla wanted to punch him. "You had no right."

"Oh, Ern," whispered Penny, who had sidled over to join them. Carla bit her tongue so hard it made her eyes water. Her mind went blank and she felt the rage boiling over. "YOU ... YOU ... TRAITOR!!!" she screamed. "You said you'd help us! GET OUT."

"Don't be crazy," said Ern. "I know it's a shock, and that you don't really know us. But we're going to help you. We owe your grandpa one. Without him, Sparks wouldn't exist this year. Besides," he said with a grin, "it's half-term – what else is there to do?" Carla stared at him. All her plans, her schemes, were fizzling out. Of course they couldn't give Grandpa a Viking funeral now; someone would tell.

"It's all over," she said.

Ern frowned. "No, Carla, it's not. . ." But Carla wasn't listening. She shook Ern off. To think that she had actually liked and trusted him. He was a rat! Carla glared at the Sparks as one by one they arrived behind the mountain. Samantha put her hand on Carla's arm. "I liked Magnus," she said quietly. "He fixed my mum's car when it broke down. He worked on it for two whole afternoons, but he wouldn't take our money. Me and Mum live on our own, and we're not very good at fixing cars. Your grandpa really helped us out."

"He was in the pub skittles team with Dad," butted in Isla. "They didn't know each other very well until Dad was accused of nicking the lifeboat charity collection box. Everyone on the skittles team turned against him, but Mr Hughes got to the bottom of it and worked out that a member of the ladies' darts team had sent off all the money to Children in Need. Mr Hughes stood by Dad during all the mud-slinging."

Bullet appeared, still dressed in his coat and hat. "He never fixed my mum's car or helped me break out of jail or anything. But he did shout at me."

"Really?" said Carla flatly. Woody flopped on Grandpa's couch. He looked sick.

"I was crossing the road without looking," admitted Bullet, "and he yelled and grabbed my shoulder and yanked me back. Then he had a massive go at me. I was only little. I was terrified. And to be straight with you, I always walked the other way if I saw him. But he probably saved my life, you know?"

Ratsy smiled and shrugged. "I'm here for a laugh, but you can trust me."

"Not because Grandpa saved your guinea pig from drowning? Or fixed your third cousin's egg timer?" asked Penny.

"Nope," said Ratsy. "None of that. I'm just in it for fun."

"He's insane," muttered Penny.

"It isn't a laugh," said Carla. "It's incredibly serious."

"I know. But this is the most exciting thing to happen in this village EVER. And I'm not going to miss out. I won't say a word to anyone, I promise." His eyes glittered with excitement.

Carla sighed. "You'd better not."

"He was your grandpa, sure," said Ern, "but he helped people. So it's only natural that we're going to want to pay him back."

"What about you?" asked Woody suddenly. "What did Grandpa do for you?"

Ern shrugged. "He said the Sparks could use his barn."

"That's not enough reason to risk being sent to prison," said Carla. "Which is what will probably happen if we are caught stealing my grandpa and setting fire to him in Gundy Bay."

"I like a challenge," said Ern, his dark eyes sparkling.

"And you need us, Carla. Why don't you try and trust us?"

"After this you're the last person I can trust," muttered Carla. But she felt a bit better. Maybe these kids could help. She didn't have any choice anyway. They were involved now. She just had to keep going.

The Sparks drifted back to work, until only Woody, Penny and Carla remained. Woody turned to Carla. "What do you think?" he asked.

"I don't know," said Carla thoughtfully. "But I think we have a chance."

"Penny?" Woody looked at his little sister.

"They've kept their mouths shut so far," Penny pointed out. "All apart from Isla. And she said she'd only mentioned it to Sophie because she thought she was bound to know already, her being your best friend."

Carla slumped on the couch next to Woody. "Sophie *was* my best friend," she said. "I don't know if she wants the job any more."

The box was large and shiny and kept slipping off her knees. Inside, Carla's carnival dress lay folded and pressed. Carla wondered if she could maybe accidently hurl it out of the window.

"You'll enjoy it once it's happening," said Mum brightly as she drove them down the country lanes to Bigwich. "I bet you'd rather be a princess at the head of the carnival than a dirty old Viking."

"No, I'd rather be a Viking," said Carla darkly.

"Never mind. It's an honour to be chosen. And I'm so proud of you." Mum squeezed her leg. "We've had such a sad time with Grandpa, but I love the way you're throwing yourself into the carnival and getting on with things. You're a real inspiration."

"Thanks," muttered Carla.

"Can I come and watch the rehearsal?"

"No," said Carla. "You won't be able to keep a straight face."

"Oh, all right," said Mum, disappointed. "I'll meet you for coffee in an hour. I need to give Maria a ring anyway. She says she's getting enormous now."

Carla felt a pang of guilt. But it was essential that nobody saw her in her costume before the big night.

As soon as Mum had dropped her at the rehearsal, Carla ducked out of the building and got out her mobile phone. She hid round the corner and dialled a number. She heard a phone ringing from an open window above her.

Carla cleared her throat, ready to do an impression of her mother.

The phone was picked up.

"Hello, this is Freya Moon, Carla's mum. I'm afraid she won't be able to make the rehearsal today. . ."

A few minutes later, Carla skipped down the street, her box tucked under her arm. It was all fixed. Now no one would see her in costume until the big night. She made for the high street. She was handing over her money in Masquerade, a fancy-dress shop, when she heard someone behind her clear their throat.

"So what is Carla Moon doing buying a blonde wig two days before her grandfather's funeral?" queried an unfriendly voice. "Don't you ever do anything normal? Shouldn't a girl your age be playing with make-up and listening to boy bands?"

Carla collected her change. "Hello to you too, Gus," she said. "What business is it of yours what I buy?" He was wearing a black T-shirt, black jeans and big black boots, and grinning in a nasty kind of way.

"You're up to something," he said. "All of you."

"It's for the carnival," said Carla, pushing past and fleeing out into the street.

"I hope it's nothing as stupid as last time," Gus shouted down the street, not caring that people were staring.

Carla spent the rest of the hour hiding in the town library then went to the café "How was it?" Mum asked. "Were the people nice?"

"It was fine," said Carla. How easy it was to slip back into lying.

"*Be careful*," said Grandpa. "*Old habits die hard.*"

"Not for ever, Grandpa," she thought. "I'll stop lying as soon as this is over."

When they got back to the car, Carla carefully folded her plastic bag so Mum wouldn't see inside. "Can you drop me at Sophie's?" She asked.

"Sure," said Mum. "I've got some time tomorrow morning and—" she paused. For a split second Carla wondered if she was going to suggest going to see the puppy.

"I wondered if you'd like me to buy you something to wear to the funeral."

Carla looked away, disappointed. "I'm not wearing black," she stated. "Grandpa wouldn't want that."

"I'm not wearing black either," said Mum. "But when I was looking through your wardrobe, I couldn't see anything suitable."

Carla sighed. She hated shopping, all the trying on of scratchy new clothes in a tiny hot cubicle with screaming kids and cackling teenagers. It was torture. But Mum was not to be thwarted.

"I'm not having you go to Grandpa's funeral in rags," she said.

"But there's so much to do for the carnival, and Grandpa wouldn't care less," repeated Carla, knowing she wasn't going to win.

"But I do," said Mum. "And I'm still here." She went quiet, and Carla realized it was one of *those* silences. Oh no, she'd done something wrong. But Mum just gave a sniff and then reached over for a hug. "I'd love to spend a morning with you, Carla sweetheart. And I promise not to make you buy anything you don't like. And we'll try to be done by lunch time. Is that a deal?"

Carla considered. Tomorrow morning the Sparks were meeting early to pull *Julie* out of the river. Then they were dividing into two teams: one in charge of costumes and the other to finish *To Valhalla!* They were going to erect the light-frame and test all the bulbs. Then they had to finish the flags and paint the dragon's head. Even now Bullet was sitting at Grandpa's table, his mother's sewing machine whirring away. He could do it at home where it was warmer, but he said it was more fun to do it in the barn.

"Please?" Mum pulled over at Sophie's house.

"All right," said Carla wearily. "If we go at ten I can do a few things with the Sparks first. Let's not go for too long, though."

Mum patted her leg. "Thanks, darling – you never know, we might even have fun."

"We might," said Carla. Shopping was never, ever fun.

The door fell open before she'd even rung the bell.

"You came then," said an accusing voice. Sophie stepped into the doorway. She was about Carla's height and build but with dark eyes, rosy cheeks and a shock of brown curly hair. "Sorry to hear about your grandpa," she said. "He was cool." Carla nodded. Sophie's voice hardened. "So what's all this about a Viking funeral then?"

"Shh," said Carla nervously. "Can we talk privately?"

Sophie led the way upstairs to her bedroom. She was going through a Goth phase. This meant her bedroom walls were painted black (Carla and Sophie had done it one afternoon when Sophie's parents were out) and she always wore black, even at school when she could get away with it. She had earrings all up her ears, and was determined to get her tongue pierced on her sixteenth birthday. She wore necklaces hanging with crucifixes and skulls and liked to spray herself liberally with patchouli perfume. She listened to Goth music and took great care to stay out of the sun, as a pale-faced complexion was part of the Goth uniform. But Sophie was naturally healthy and pink-cheeked. This annoyed her and so she plastered her face in white make-up. With all this in mind Carla had been surprised at her friend's desire to be this year's Carnival Princess, where the wearing of a pink dress, tiara and pearls was obligatory.

"It's all about drama," Sophie had explained. "We Goths love drama and dressing theatrically." Now Sophie sat on her black bed and leaned against her black walls. "Come on," she said, when Carla had closed the door. "What's going on?" Carla decided to start right at the beginning with the finding of Grandpa's letter. She spoke about how Ern had overheard them, and how he had told the Sparks. "I didn't tell you," said Carla, "because I didn't know they all knew, and I was worried that the more people knew, the more likely it was that it would get stopped."

"But I'm supposed to be your best friend," said Sophie. "You made me feel really left out."

"Sorry," said Carla truthfully. "I got so caught up in it all; I didn't stop to think about anyone else's feelings."

But Sophie was grinning. "You crazy fool," she said.

"This is just up my street. How can I help?"

"Actually, there is something only you can do." Carla hesitated. If what she said next went down badly, she could lose her friend for life. She had to tread very carefully. "I'm going to suggest something, but you have to promise you won't hate me for it," said Carla.

"I can't promise that. Come on, out with it," ordered Sophie. "Do you want me to be a Viking? Drive the tractor? Help you steal your grandpa?"

"None of those," said Carla, getting out the blonde wig. "Just try this on."

Julie

Thursday was another cold blustery day. It seemed that the hedges and trees had lost all their leaves all at once. The grass was muddy and damp and there weren't any flowers anywhere. All the Sparks, bar one, were assembled on the riverbank watching *Julie* gently bobbing in the current. They had all agreed that the only way to cover *Valkyrie*'s disappearance, albeit temporarily, was to get *Julie* in carnival condition so when *Valkyrie* was burned, *Julie* could take her place doing the rounds of the other carnivals. Carla felt lucky to be surrounded by a group of such cool people. No one had objected to the extra work. But one of the Sparks was missing. "We'll have to start without him," said Carla, fed up that Ern was late. She was supposed to be meeting Mum in half an hour for the dreaded shopping trip, and they wouldn't get another opportunity to do this. Dad had gone to work and Mum was busy organizing funeral things. Carla gambled that neither of them would notice *Julie* was missing for ages.

Julie was moored to the wooden jetty close to Grandpa's gate. A little way upstream there was a narrow slipway, which was mostly mud and weeds. Carla hoped they'd be able to pull *Julie* out here. There were a lot of them; surely it could be done? Once *Julie* was on dry land, Carla was planning to roll her up to the barn, using round wooden stakes as rollers.

Isla stepped down the bank to the jetty and tied a new line to *Julie*'s nose. She then passed the end of the rope to Carla, who fed it along the group until everyone was holding on. Then Isla untied the rope at the stern and *Julie* swung round sideways, out into the river. Isla was about to untie the painter at the stem of the boat when she hesitated. "This might not work," she called. "She looks heavy."

"It'll be fine," said Carla impatiently.

"OK," said Isla. She untied the painter. "Now," she shouted, and the children leaned back with the rope as *Julie* floated free. Carla immediately felt a strong pull, which dragged the line of children a few paces towards the river. Isla joined the end of the line, heaving and tugging, but it was hard work and the children couldn't haul *Julie* any closer to the bank. She was too heavy and the current was too strong.

"It's all the rain," called Isla. "It's made the river faster than usual."

"Oh, help," whispered Carla. They were being

tugged further and further along the bank away from the slipway. Carla, sweating, was closest to the water. As her feet slipped in the mud, she realized the danger. Bullet had been pulled right over twice already. She ordered the littlest ones to stay back, and told Penny to go and get the lifebelt from its stand, just in case.

"We need to tie her up," shouted Woody. "We can't hold her."

Carla knew he was right, but they'd travelled too far down the riverbank. The rope wasn't long enough. Helplessly she felt herself being towed with the current as they all heaved and strained. But what could they do? If they weren't careful, they'd be dragged to the bend, where the current gained pace, and the Dugg joined the River Wich. Then they'd lose her for ever. Carla gripped the rope so hard her fingers turned white.

"There!" shouted Woody, pointing downstream to a fat tree stump poking out of the dead nettles on the edge of the bank.

"OK," called Carla, trying not to sound as panicky as she felt. "New plan: secure the line to that stump." The children slithered along the bank to the spot and Isla hurried to the end of the rope and tied a knot, making *Julie* fast. Everyone was panting and comparing rope burns. Carla was flooded with relief that *Julie* was secure. But the boat was bobbing round in the current at an odd angle. What if she was caught up in something? What if she sank? How was Carla ever going to explain all this to her parents? She looked round in alarm as a *phut-phut* noise came from a nearby gateway. A tractor pulled through and parked on the riverbank. An elderly man sat grinning in the driver's seat, and a figure dashed out in front.

"Where've you been?" screeched Carla as Ern galloped up to her. "We nearly lost *Julie*. We needed you."

Ern looked at the boat, jostled by the water, with splashes breaking over the stem. "Barney will pull her out." He ran back to talk to the old man before Carla could say anything. She bit her lip as the tractor reversed slowly down the path. Ern got out a chain and helped Isla to secure the line to it. "It's going to make a mess," he called. "But better than losing the boat." He told the Sparks to stand back. They all cheered as, at a nod from Ern, Barney edged forward, and *Julie* moved against the current back up the river.

"She's going over!" shrieked Carla as *Julie* lurched and wobbled. But somehow she didn't; she turned round so her stem was, at last, facing forward, and she nosed the bank. A few minutes later she was slithering up the mud slipway and gleaming on the bank like a big wet monster.

Barney switched the engine off. "Want me to take her over to Magnus's barn?" he called. He had a thick Somerset accent. "Got a trailer in the next field. Or I could haul her on to a tarpaulin and just drag her there."

Carla watched dumbly as the Sparks huddled round Barney discussing the best way to get *Julie* into the barn.

"Was this part of your plan?" asked Penny brightly.

"Shut up," said Carla, sucking her raw fingers and eyeing old Barney. Did he know everything too? She knew she had messed up, and even though Ern had saved the day, she was mad at him. If he'd been here earlier and hadn't gone behind her back *again*, maybe, just maybe, they could have pulled *Julie* out by themselves.

She was late, of course. Mum was sitting at the kitchen table, dressed in her coat and fiddling with her handbag, when Carla burst in. "Sorry," said Carla, panting. She'd run all the way back, not knowing whether they'd got *Julie* in the barn or not. Ern said they'd manage just fine and she didn't need to worry about Barney. Carla had just shaken her head. At this rate, half the village would know her secret before Friday.

"I wanted to collect you but you insisted on no visitors," said Mum. "Come on; let's not waste any more time." An hour and half later and Carla was itching to get back to work on *To Valhalla!* Every time Mum showed her a skirt or a top, Carla just nodded her head and said, "Maybe." She glanced at her watch. If Mum was true to her word, they'd be finished in twenty minutes even though neither of them had bought a thing. But then, in the millionth shop, just as Carla had shrugged at a swishy scarlet skirt Mum was showing her (which was quite nice, but Carla really couldn't be bothered to do up all the fiddly buttons), her mother slumped. She put her hand to her head and her shoulders starting shaking. Carla clicked into the present. "What's wrong?" She looked at her mother and was alarmed to see she was crying, again.

"I hadn't imagined shopping for clothes for Dad's funeral," sniffed Mum. "And this is hard work. You don't want to be here. I'd hoped we might have some *fun* together."

"Oh, Mum," said Carla. She stepped forward and gave her a hug. "I'm sorry." Several other shoppers were looking at them curiously.

"You're always distracted," sighed Mum. "Since Grandpa died, it's like you're not here at all. I know you're sad. Maybe this is your way of dealing with it?" Carla didn't know what to say.

"I really wanted . . . oh, I don't know." Mum wiped a tear from the end of her nose. "Shall we go for a hot chocolate?" she suggested in a shaky voice.

Carla couldn't help looking at her watch. If they went for a drink now, they'd then have a late lunch at home. And that would mean a late start to the afternoon's work. "All right," she said, trying to sound enthusiastic. She felt sorry for Mum, but there was so much to do!

Mum looked at her. "You're just humouring me.

Come on, let's go home. You can wear your brown skirt and red blouse to the funeral. I'll iron them for you. I've got enough to do at home without wasting any more time here." Weariness had settled in her voice.

"Mum, I. . ." Carla felt remorse. She should have made more effort.

"Don't worry," snapped Mum. They made their way back to the car in silence.

Carla stepped into the silent barn. Everyone had been invited back to Bullet's house for lunch. It was nice to have the place to herself. When she was alone in here it felt like Grandpa could come walking in through the door. She lifted the tarpaulin to look at *Julie*, sitting on Barney's trailer. She needed a scrub to remove the slime. She brought a dank, musty smell into the barn. Carla let the tarpaulin drop and went over to Grandpa's workbench to examine the dragon figurehead. They weren't going to burn it with *Valkyrie*. There was no time, Isla said, to make two.

And here was Napoleon. What would become of him? Carla reached up and felt around the old bear's neck. His fur was stiff with dirt and he smelled mouldy. His glass eyes were dusty. He looked very dead.

"Maybe it's time you went, old bear," said Carla. She cringed as a tiny yellow beetle ran over the fur of his chest. It wouldn't be long before he fell into dust. Her eyes narrowed as she looked at him. Maybe she could find a use for him. She grabbed the metal stool and dragged it over to the stuffed bear. Balancing on one leg, she reached round and felt the back of Napoleon's neck. She found the loose flap of fur and drew out the box. Carla sat on Grandpa's couch and took out a small wad of envelopes tied with grey string. The first letter was written in an italic scrawl Carla found hard to read.

Magnus,

I am furious. How could you! You have ruined both our chances of a happy life together. . .

Carla didn't know what she'd been expecting, but it wasn't this.

You are a selfish, useless, fickle man. I'm only glad I found out about the depths of your depravity BEFORE I married you. Now you've got another wedding to arrange, HAVE YOU NOT? Or have you become completely dishonourable?

I'm heartbroken and furious. I shall never speak to you again.

You have broken my heart.

J

Who was this woman J? Grandpa had never mentioned her. Carla unfolded the next letter. The postmark was a few months later than the first.

Magnus,

You have to stop badgering me and marry the poor girl. I will have nothing more to do with you. I have many new suitors now, though none are as ugly as you.

J

PS I never told you, but I can't swim. And I know the contempt you have for non-swimmers. So it would never have worked anyway.

This J person obviously didn't hate Grandpa as much as she said she did. The next letter came three months later.

Magnus Hughes,

At least you've done something right at last.

But I am still SO CROSS about how stupid you were. Just because you sail away for a year doesn't mean you can behave like you did. I'll never forgive you.

Do not send me any more letters. It is not seemly or kind to your new wife.

Best wishes,

J

Carla heard the door creak and a foot step and she stuffed the letters back in the envelope.

"Carla?"

She stood up. It was only Ern. She put the box in her bag. There was one letter left to read. "Over here," she called, and came out to meet him. Ern was looking tired. He had dark smudges under his eyes and he was wearing this morning's dirty checked shirt.

"We could never have pulled *Julie* out of the river without a tractor," he said gently. "And I knew you wouldn't allow Barney to help. So I went ahead and asked him anyway. We can trust Barney. Are you still mad at me?"

"Probably," said Carla wearily. She didn't know what to make of Ern any more. She was fed up with him running around and doing things behind her back. But, she had to admit, her plan to land *Julie* would never have worked without him. Ern was rubbing his face in a worried kind of way. Just then a shaft of sunlight poured in through the window. Grandpa's crystals spun on their strings and the barn became alive with dancing rainbows. They stood for a minute, watching the lights dance over the thick stone walls and fly over the floor.

"Grandpa loved rainbows," said Carla, perching on a tyre. "He would always make us go outside to look at them. He said they were proof that magic existed."

"He was special," said Ern, sitting next to her. He paused. Uh-oh, thought Carla. He's going to drop another bombshell.

"The thing is," said Ern, "some of the kids have been talking. None of us wants to bother you, because of your grandpa. . ." He pulled awkwardly at his sleeve. "But, Carla, you need to tell us about your plans, about the practicalities. How are we going to get Magnus from

147

Mr Salt's? How are we going to launch and burn him? How are we going to make sure he doesn't come back in on the tide? And how are we going to stop everyone finding out what we have done?" He smiled at her encouragingly. "It doesn't matter if you haven't got all the answers. Maybe I can help you. We're all in this together, but you have to let me know. There's not much time left."

Carla felt cornered. "I'll come clean," she said. "I've got plans for some of it, only they're best kept quiet. I'll tell you things if you promise to keep your mouth shut."

Ern nodded. "Sure." He grinned. "You can trust me. Look at my track record."

Carla frowned. "But I must admit, I might need some help. Everyone expects me to have all the answers, but I don't." Her voice broke and she turned away, not wanting to see the expression on Ern's face.

"So what do we need to sort out?" he enquired brightly.

Carla sighed. "I'm still not completely sure how I'm going to get into Mr Salt's funeral parlour, but I know the alarm code."

Ern looked amused. "How?"

"I just do, so I'm not worried about the alarm going off. I just need to know how I'm going to break in. I've never broken in anywhere. Have you?"

Ern shook his head. "Wasn't Mr Salt a friend of your grandpa's?" he asked. "Isn't there some way we could persuade him to—"

"I know what you're going to say," interrupted Carla. "Mr Salt was friends with Grandpa for years, but if he gets involved with stealing a body, he could get sent to prison. He'd be ruined. We can't ask him to take that risk."

"So what are we going to do?" asked Ern.

Carla liked how he said "we" and not "you". It was hard to stay cross with him for long. And she liked him in his red-and-black checked shirt and jeans. He looked older. He had a smudge of dirt on his cheek. He obviously hadn't looked in the mirror this morning. Come to think of it, neither had she. She rubbed at the corners of her eyes, to check for eye-bogeys.

"And how will we know we've got your grandpa, and not someone else?" asked Ern nervously.

"The coffins are labelled," said Carla. "Look, if anything goes wrong, we can pull out. The main thing is that we try." She explained her alternative plan, which involved going to visit Grandpa on Friday but *not leaving*. She'd get all three of them, Woody, Penny and herself, to go to the funeral parlour. They'd tell Mum they wanted to go on their own. During the visit Carla would have to find somewhere to hide, and she knew just the place: the coffin storage room. It made her shiver to even to think about it. Carla really, really hoped she wouldn't have to do this. This plan was much more risky. She'd have to lay lots of lies to cover her absence. Of course, once everyone had left, there was nothing to stop her coming out of the coffin room, collecting Grandpa and letting herself out.

"It's pretty shaky," said Ern.

"We'll need superpowers to do it," Carla muttered. "Grandpa would say I should go up to Iron Knoll and drink some water from the spring. Then I'll have special powers for twenty-four hours."

"I could do with some of that," said Ern. "Let's go and get some now."

"You are joking! We've got so much to do here, and the rest of the Sparks will be here in a minute. . ."

"We'll go on our bikes," said Ern. "We need all the help we can get."

They left their bikes at the bottom of the hill and puffed up the steep slope. Carla's leg muscles burned as they climbed higher and higher. It was a dull, breezy day, and up here the wind was even stronger. As they climbed, Carla told Ern about her disastrous shopping trip with Mum.

"She's not mad with you, she's sad about Magnus," said Ern. But Carla wasn't so sure. She also told him about her plan for substituting the coffins and for making sure Grandpa sank once he was right out in the channel.

"We could stop at the barn on the way to the sea and pick up Grandpa's old anchor and sea chains," she said. "That should weigh down whatever doesn't burn."

"But how do you know he'll go out far enough?" panted Ern.

Carla told him about the test run, and how the launch would take place as the tide was turning. "Grandpa also has a small outboard motor he was planning to attach to *Valkyrie*," said Carla. "The fittings are already in place on the transom; we just need to screw it on."

"I can see where this is going," said Ern. "You want to wedge the motor on and set her off."

Carla stopped for a breather. "I'd rather not," she puffed. "It's not the sort of thing that should end up on the seabed. But we might have to."

"You won't have to," said Ern. "Isla says once the boat gets into the tide race it will go right out. But the motor thing wouldn't work. You'd need someone to drive it."

From up here Carla could see Gundy beach, the car park and the war platform. She planned to launch the boat a little further up the beach from where they'd had the practice run. From here it should be swept right out into the water, where it would hopefully sink in the deepest part of the channel. Carla looked out at the grey sea. A dark fog swirled low over the water as a vast container ship slid up the channel. She hoped there wouldn't be anything like that on the sea on Friday night. It could complicate things. She watched the cars beetle up and down the motorway. To her left, she saw Bigwich in all its grey glory, and beyond that the snaking estuary and her own village.

"I'm a bit worried about the mud," she admitted. "We'll have to push the boat out quite a way before the current takes her. And we nearly drowned coming back on our test run."

Ern gazed at her. "That is a problem," he agreed. "We need two boats."

"Or a mud horse," said Carla. "You know, those wooden ski things Ernie uses to cart his fishing equipment out over the mud without sinking."

Ern frowned and then brightened. "It might work," he said. "Come on, I'll race you to the top. It looks like we need those special powers more than ever." He raced off up the path and Carla scrambled up the steep hill after him. She was breathing hard when she reached the top. The summit of Iron Knoll was flat, like someone had sliced the top off the hill like a boiled egg. She felt curiously elated. Up here all her worries seemed to fly away.

The spring trickled out of the gap between two large flattish slabs of grey stone. The water was quickly swallowed up in the mossy damp ground. Ern squatted, his hair tousled by the wind. "What are we waiting for?" He cupped his hands under the trickle and then put it to his mouth and swallowed. "Notice anything?" he asked, turning to Carla. "Have I got a glow or something?"

"Grandpa said you needed to drink a whole cup for it to work," said Carla. So Ern scooped more and more water into his mouth. Then he roared and ran off, whooping and howling. Carla grinned. She crouched by the spring and tasted the water. It was very cold, and a faintly metallic flavour filled her mouth. She drank more. She didn't feel any different. She looked out over the bay. A mist had risen and there was a vivid band of colours hanging in the sky – a sea rainbow. Grandpa so loved rainbows.

"Grandpa?" A figure was coming out of the mist, a tall, rangy silhouette. But it was only Ern.

"One. Two. Three," he said with a serious expression. "One. Two. Three."

"One, two three, what?" asked Carla, dreamily watching the rainbow fade into the mist. Ern stood next to her.

"One, two, three." He sighed. "One, two, three, *four*."

And to her surprise, he kissed her.

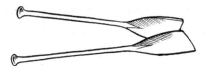

The Plan

It was a good first kiss. No, Carla decided, it was better than that. It was magic. Sophie said kissing Justin Fletcher had been like snogging a fish, all wet and blubbery. But Ern's mouth had felt soft and warm. After just a couple of seconds he'd let her go and grinned at her and said he'd only been brave enough to do it because he had superpowers.

When they got back, Grandpa's barn was full of Sparks. Ratsy rushed in, wearing a plastic Viking helmet.

"Intruder!" he yelped. Quickly the children hauled the tarpaulin over *Julie*. Then they pulled *Valkyrie* to the centre of the barn. Then, apart from Isla, who had been cleaning muck out of *Julie*, they resumed work. It wouldn't do for prying eyes to see that two boats, not one, were being transformed.

There was a timid knock at the door.

"No entry," said Ern sternly. "This is a members-only enclosure."

"It's me," said a timid voice.

Carla rushed over. "It's OK," she said. "Let her in." Everyone stared as Sophie walked in, wearing a long black dress that trailed over the floor. "Everyone, you probably know Sophie. She's our secret weapon." She grinned at her. Sophie looked in wonder at *Valkyrie*. The dragon head was finished and curved up from the stem. They'd set the sails, and striped flags (triangles cut from several pairs of Ratsy's dad's pyjamas) hung from the mast and sprit. Three sets of oars had been placed strategically down the boat.

"She's lovely!" gasped Sophie. She looked at Carla. "You're not really going to burn her?"

Carla nodded.

"What a shame." Secretly Carla agreed. But she couldn't think about that now. She showed Sophie all over the boat, and Bullet allowed her to examine the costumes. Then Carla hauled off the tarpaulin to expose *Julie*.

"What's this for?" asked Sophie, wrinkling her nose. *Julie* was still rather smelly.

"That's the clever part," said Carla, and explained how Julie would take *Valkyrie*'s place after she was burned. Then Sophie got stuck in, helping Samantha paint the shields. These were six wooden discs Samantha's dad had made for them. The Sparks were going to string them along the sides of the boat. Carla watched as Isla went out to take Ratsy's place on sentry duty. Penny was busy blasting *Julie* with a hairdryer in an attempt to dry her out so they could paint her. Woody looked up and smiled. Carla smiled back. She hoped she wasn't going to let them all down.

Ern had gone to the beach. He'd borrowed the cart and was ferrying sandbags to the concrete war platform. In amongst the sandbags he had also concealed several gallons of paraffin, stolen from Isla's garage, and five big cardboard boxes full of packets of firelighters. (These had been the most expensive part of the whole project so far, and he'd had to despatch Barney to buy them.) He was also going to check out Barney's mud horses, to see if they might safely transport the children back over the mud in the ebbing tide on Friday night. Penny appeared at her side. "Mum was crying again after lunch," she said quietly.

"Grandpa just died." Carla frowned. "It's no wonder she's crying."

"Maybe we should tell her what we're doing," Penny said, not looking at her sister. "She might like to come along."

"No," said Carla. "It would ruin everything." She felt hot and cold. It was as if the ground was falling away beneath her. She couldn't believe what Penny was suggesting. It would mean the whole thing was over, wouldn't it?

A little later, when Ern was back, Carla called a meeting. Everyone sat on a tyre. Carla didn't say anything, but she didn't like the tyre mountain being taken apart. It meant that Grandpa's couch was in full view.

But she could hear him now. *"Don't sweat the small stuff."*

She cleared her throat and rearranged her notes. Then she spread a large map of Bigwich town centre over the floor.

"OK, we have to assemble at Broadway tomorrow at six p.m., ready for kick-off at seven. We're quite far back in the line-up so we might not leave the parade until half past. Mr Blake is driving the tractor, so he'll be here to hitch up *To Valhalla!* at five. You'll join us – in costume – at Broadway. The leading carts finish at ten; we finish some time after." Carla looked around the group. She had a feeling some of them were lost already.

"All the carts are parked back in Broadway ready for the squibbing walk and firework display. It's during this time Mr Blake traditionally goes off to watch the squibbing, then to the pub. This is when those of us who can get away can take the tractor, pick up Grandpa and drive to the sea. We need to be there at high tide, which is midnight. Is everyone clear about what is going to happen?"

From the puzzled faces, this was clearly not the case.

"I've got a question," piped up Bullet. "Who is going to drive the tractor to the sea? None of us are old enough."

"Me" said Ern firmly. "I've been driving tractors since I was four years old. I'll be fine. And I know where Dad keeps the spare keys."

"But won't the police stop us when they see a kid driving it?" asked Bullet.

"I've got a grey wig," said Ern. "It's foolproof. Besides, we've still got to decorate the tractor. I intend to put a large Viking shield over the top of the windscreen, with slits to see out. Very often you can't see the driver in carnival parades."

"What if we get caught?" said Isla.

"If I get caught driving a tractor and trailer containing the body of Magnus Hughes, I think I'm going to have rather more to explain than why I'm driving my dad's tractor on the night of the carnival," said Ern.

"And what will your dad say when he sees the tractor is missing?" asked Woody anxiously.

Ern shrugged. "I'll say I thought he'd had too much to drink so I drove it back myself." He made it all sound very plausible, but everyone knew he was sticking his neck out. "The trailer tips," Ern went on. "I have to drive it through the dunes and over the hard sand to the water, then gently slide out *Valkyrie* and Mr Hughes. I'll need lots of help arranging the sandbags and helping with the fuel. Whoever is coming needs a watertight alibi."

"I won't be there," said Bullet gloomily. "My mum will take me home after the carnival. She's even going to walk by the side all the way."

"Can't you say you're staying at our house?" suggested Isla.

"My mum is mates with yours; she'll find out the truth sooner or later," said Bullet. "She always does." He pulled at his lower lip.

"Then you'll have to be our man in HQ," said Ern. "We'll get you a mobile and you can be on alert in case of unforeseen circumstances."

That night the children sat around the kitchen table hardly saying a word. Each was deep in their thoughts. Mum looked around at them all.

"Since Grandpa died, I've hardly seen anything of you. I don't know if that's good or bad." Nobody replied. "Can I get a sneak preview?" she asked. "I'd love to see what's been taking up all your time."

"Don't cheat, Freya," said Dad through a mouthful of sausage. "They seem to be doing well without us. We can wait another day."

"I suppose so." Mum rolled her sausage round her plate. "But it's been a lonely week." She suddenly smiled. "Once we've got through this weekend, let's go and see that puppy. I'd completely forgotten about it."

"Yes!" shouted Woody, jumping up and knocking his plate to the floor. Carla felt a flood of happiness. But then she saw Penny raising her eyebrow at her and it struck her.

If Mum found out what they were going to do with Grandpa, it would be very unlikely they'd be getting a puppy, ever.

It was raw and rainy outside – a night where the only sensible option was to stay in bed. But Carla crept across the landing, grimacing as the floorboards creaked. She waited a few seconds to make sure she hadn't woken anyone, then pushed open Woody's door and tiptoed in.

"I'd hoped you were Grandpa's ghost," said a matter-of-fact voice from the bed. "Coming to tell me not to worry about the Viking funeral after all. And that a normal burial in the churchyard would be just fine, thank you."

"You're not having second thoughts, are you?" asked Carla.

"Carla," said Woody, sitting up and turning on his night light, "I've had second, third, fourth, fifth and sixth thoughts about this."

"Me too," said Carla. She didn't mention her worries about the puppy. It might tip her brother over the edge. She got out Grandpa's letters from her dressing-gown pocket. "Look at these." She watched him whilst he read, scratching his head every now and then.

"But who is J?" he asked eventually. "I've never heard of him."

"Her, not him," said Carla. "She's someone from Grandpa's past. I've still got one more to read."

Magnus,
So your daughter has been born. (I read about it in the paper.) Congratulations. I am happy for you.

160

I know you always wanted a little girl. I can even
guess what you will call her. Look after your little
Freya. Now don't drown, and I'll think of you,
sometimes bitter, sometimes sweet.

Yours ever (and for God's sake burn these letters),
J

"But what's it all about?" asked Woody. Carla thought he looked very small, sitting up in bed in his Batman pyjamas.

"Grown-up stuff," said Carla. "Remember we always wondered why he married Grandma when she was such an old bag? Well, maybe he didn't mean to marry her. Maybe he *had* to marry her."

"Oh," Woody looked blank.

"He really wanted to marry this J," said Carla, wondering if she was going to have to spell it all out, "but Grandma bagged him first."

"How?" asked Woody.

"Love stuff," said Carla.

"Oh, right," said Woody hurriedly. Then, "Carla, did you have to come and show me this now? Couldn't it wait? It's a big day tomorrow."

"I couldn't sleep," said Carla. "And I knew you, Mr Insomniac, wouldn't be asleep either. Besides, our work isn't over."

Woody groaned. "I knew there had to be more to it," he said. "What do you want me to do now?"

*

The cold hit them like a bucket of freezing water. Carla pulled her hat low down over her ears and a shiver went all the way through her.

"Oh God," said Woody as they gently shut the kitchen door. "When do I learn to say no to you?"

"Shh, you'll wake everyone up." The children crept down the garden to the river. When they were out of view of the house they flicked on their torches. "If you see anything move – anything   turn the torch off," ordered Carla. "I hope it's not like this tomorrow night." The wind blew hard and chilled them to the core, though they still had their pyjamas on under their clothes. Rain hit them hard in the face. Grandpa's barn was in darkness. Carla couldn't risk switching on the lights so they had to make do with their torches. Ern's dad had come that afternoon to finally secure *To Valhalla!* to the trailer.

"It wouldn't do for her to go sailing off into the crowd, now would it?" he'd chuckled, as he ratcheted fast the webbing which was strapped over *Valkyrie*'s hull. Personally Carla thought Mr Blake had gone a bit over the top with the attachments. Each new rope, each bracket he erected, made her worry. How were they going to get it all off in time?

"Now she's safe," he'd said, patting the hull. Carla had made a note to add a very sharp knife to the things she needed to leave at the beach.

Grandpa said, *"If in doubt, put your head down and just keep moving forward."*

"Is it really high tide at midnight tomorrow?" asked Woody, shivering. His breath clouded out between his chattering teeth.

"Yes," said Carla. "And the moon should still be quite big. If it's a clear night, we won't need any torches."

"We'll be seen for miles and miles," said Woody. He wiped mud off his handlebars. "Come on, let's get this over with. I want to go back to bed."

The beach was grey and unwelcoming. An easterly wind whipped the waves along the shore. The children were cold to the bone. Carla's fingers didn't work properly as she pulled back the sandbags and deposited yet more firelighters, a rope, Mum's sharpest kitchen knife, four boxes of matches and an emergency flare swiped from *Julie's* locker.

"What's that for?" asked Woody.

"Just in case," said Carla mysteriously. She hadn't forgotten the mud. It would be good to have some kind of distress signal if things went wrong. They went to look at old Barney's mud horses.

"Are these really going to save us from drowning?" said Woody sceptically, looking at the old wooden contraptions.

"It's what they're made for," said Carla. "It's either use these, or just push Grandpa out very close to the shore and hope for the best. But mud horses or not, we mustn't go out as deep as last time. That was too scary. And you don't have to come at all. Me and Ern can do it."

"We'll see about that," muttered Woody, looking at the dark water.

They squelched through the mud, over the bank and back to their dirty bicycles. Not for the first time, Carla wondered if a nice church burial, with grass and earth and flowers and relatives, wouldn't be a better idea than an illegal funeral, alone but for some children and the howling sea. She glanced back at the water. Far off in the distance, across the channel, the lights of Wales twinkled. This time tomorrow they would be doing it! They cycled home in the wind and rain. No one was about. This was good, Carla thought. There wasn't likely to be anyone about tomorrow night either.

At home the children crept through the back door and into the house. Everything was deathly quiet. Nelson opened his one, disapproving, eye and watched them as they crept through the kitchen and up the stairs. Carla gave Woody a nod and they tiptoed their separate ways back to their bedrooms. Long ago they had worked out how to walk in sync, so that the creaking floorboards wouldn't give them away when they were both up and about at night. They made it back to their rooms undetected. Carla didn't sleep properly at all that night. She had dream after dream – sinking in quicksand, or Penny and Woody shrinking to the size of mice and getting lost. Carla woke up between each dream and, looking at the luminous numbers on her alarm clock, would see time had barely moved. It always seemed to be some time in the region of three a.m.

"*I find most things turn out OK*," said Grandpa, "*but only if you use your loaf.*"

Carla groaned and opened her eyes. Four-thirty. At last it was nearly morning. She got out of bed. Maybe she should just give up on sleep. She went to her window and looked out at the dark garden. The sky had cleared and she could see the stars twinkling in the heavens. Beyond the garden hedge she saw the river gleam.

Today was the day.

A Bit of a Rest

By eight-thirty everyone was already at work. Bullet handed out the costumes and Samantha helped people put them on, making adjustments here and there. Ratsy was busy cutting out a large square of tarpaulin to cover the generator in case it rained, and Ern and Isla were tying the wooden waves to the sides of the trailer.

"Tacky," said Penny, looking at the result, "but effective."

They were planning to reuse a lot of stuff for *Julie*. There was no point, for example, in burning the waves, or the flags, or the shields, and Isla forbade Carla to burn the oars.

"Dad would murder me," she said. Carla was concerned again that once *Valkyrie* was stripped of these things, it would make her look very bare for Grandpa.

"He wouldn't mind," said Woody, when she asked him what he thought. "Besides, we don't have a choice." There was a sense of urgency and excitement as everyone got on with their jobs. Isla was now busy with carnival paperwork, and Penny was putting last-minute touches to the row of horned helmets which stood on Grandpa's workbench.

"If it rains, they'll melt," she said.

Woody rummaged in an old chest and eventually pulled out three bright orange life vests. Carla watched as he shoved these in the back of the trailer, behind the generator.

"What are those for?" she asked.

"You're not the only one who gets letters," said Woody, and that was all he would say on the matter. Carla eyed him speculatively. What else had Grandpa arranged?

All too soon, the morning was over and Carla reluctantly had to leave. She had to trust that everyone would do their allotted tasks.

"We're going to do it," said Ern, reading her thoughts. "There's no reason why our plan should fail."

"There are a million reasons why it should fail," observed Penny. "But none of them will stop my sister."

Dad and Carla were the only visitors to the funeral parlour that morning. Idly Carla watched Rowan polish the hearse outside.

"Mum said to say goodbye for her," said Dad, tapping

his knees. "After this visit, they're going to seal the coffin." He looked at her. "I'm more nervous than you," he said. "Look at you – you're as cool as a cucumber." Carla nodded, only half listening. She certainly wasn't feeling cool. She was terrified. How was she going to sneak into the preparation room and steal the keys?

"You wouldn't believe the amount of organization that has to go into a funeral," said Dad, shifting on his chair. "You kids have had it easy; messing around with your carnival float must help take your minds off it. But your mum and I are in the thick of it."

"Oh yeah?" murmured Carla.

"We're going to need a holiday after all the work we've done," said Dad.

Mr Salt appeared. "Magnus is ready, if you are," he said, *putting his keys on the table.* Carla couldn't tear her eyes away.

"Are you sure you want to see him again?" asked Dad. "You don't have to. He wouldn't mind."

"You go first," said Carla. "I'll join you in a minute."

Dad gave her arm a squeeze. "I'll see you in there, then." He stood and straightened his trousers. "Lead the way," he said in an unnaturally bright voice, and Mr Salt opened the door into the chapel of rest. Carla's head was pounding as she stared at the keys. But now the phone was ringing and Mr Salt was back. "Excuse me one moment," he was saying. He picked up the receiver.

"Yes, yes, I see. . . No, I wouldn't mind a cat. But they're not easy to predict. Was she adamant?" Mr Salt paced up and down the room and when he passed her, he gave Carla the smallest wink. Then he picked the keys up and put them in his jacket pocket. Carla felt her spirits plummet. So close. She'd have to sneak into the prep room after all.

"Of course she can have mahogany. . ."

Carla waited, her heart thumping. She looked at the fish in the aquarium, hoping for inspiration. If she couldn't get the keys, she'd have to go to plan B. She shivered at the prospect. She'd got her mobile phone so she could send a text from inside the coffin room, where she would have to hide. She knew what she was going to say.

HI DAD. CHANGED MY MIND. GONE TO SOPHIE'S.

And a few hours later she was going to text again:
STAYING AT SOPH'S FOR TEA. C U LATER!

But now she was faced with it she really, really didn't want to go in that coffin room and hide. It was too creepy. Mr Salt finished his conversation, took his jacket off, draped it over his chair and walked off down the corridor and into the prep room. The door closed behind him with a swish. In an instant Carla crossed the room and started fumbling through the pockets. She found two humbugs, a piece of paper explaining about death duties, a lottery ticket and two sets of keys. One set was obviously car keys, so she put those back, but there was a key ring, and on the key ring were two keys. They both had labels attached. One said "spare main door". The other said "prep". Carla wound these off the key fob, pinching her thumb in the process as her hands were shaking so much. Then she took a deep breath and slipped into the chapel of rest.

"We thought you were never coming," said Dad, sitting by the far wall. "We thought you'd lost your nerve."

"We?" said Carla, fingering the key in her pocket.

"Me and your grandpa," said Dad, smiling.

Carla studied Grandpa. He looked even smaller than before. She blinked. There had been something. No. She wasn't sure. But she could have sworn that for an instant she had seen the ghost of a smile on his lips. It must be the light; it was so dark and gloomy in here. Grandpa didn't look much like Grandpa any more. He was too pale, too empty, too still. Carla shivered.

"He's really gone," said Dad, echoing her thoughts.

"I'm going to do it, Grandpa," Carla said in her head. "Tonight is the night. Do you still want us to do this?"

Grandpa's reply came without any pause at all. Here in her head he was as alive as ever.

"Of course I do, my beautiful. I'm very proud of you. But remember, there are always surprises when you least expect them. And don't do anything dangerous. Don't go out on the mud. Launch the boat from the shore. The tide and the wind will catch me."

Carla paused. She'd have to see about that. "I miss you, Grandpa."

"*I miss you too, sweetheart. But I wouldn't have wanted to grow old and weak. I wouldn't like to have to depend on others for everything. I've got out before the rot set in,*"

"But I wouldn't have minded looking after you, Grandpa."

"*Age is a terrible thing, darling. You can't fight it. Inside you still feel twenty-five, but as you get older, your body starts to hurt. After a while, you look forward to a rest.*"

"Is this what this is, Grandpa? A bit of a rest?"

"*That's right.*"

"Will I ever see you again, Grandpa?"

Carla waited. Was he ever going to reply? But then he whispered in a sad voice, totally unlike his own, "*No, darling.*"

Carla kissed his cold, lifeless cheek, and a tear plopped on his face. A sob escaped her, and her eyes went blurry with tears.

"Goodbye, Grandpa," she whispered. "Goodbye."

Dad took her hand, and without speaking they walked out of the room. Carla didn't turn round. She couldn't bear it.

Maria's Baby

Outside, Dad hugged Carla so hard her ribs nearly cracked. When he stepped away she saw he too had tears in his eyes. "I don't know if I'm sadder about you being sad or about Grandpa," he said. "I'm double sad."

"Sorry," said Carla, as tears dribbled down her face. Dad hugged her again. Then they drove home. Carla couldn't stop thinking about how that was the last time she was ever going to see Grandpa. She'd never see his face again. Never. This wasn't sad. This was AWFUL. Each time she thought she'd stopped crying, she'd start shaking and sniffing all over again. And she had so much to do! Why had she broken down now, of all times? But she couldn't stop herself. She just wanted to curl up somewhere dark and quiet.

"You know what?" said Dad.

"What?" Carla could barely see, her eyes were so swollen.

"It's wonderful that you loved him so much. The sadder you feel, the more you loved him. That's beautiful."

Carla thought about this.

"It's wonderful for a person to be loved. That's all you can ask."

Carla sighed deeply and fingered the keys in her pocket. Yes, she loved Grandpa all right. And now she was going to give him the funeral he deserved.

At home everyone seemed to have a million and one things to do. Mum was ironing all their clothes for the next day and trying to talk on the telephone at the same time. Woody was already dressed in his Viking costume and furiously searching the house for an extension lead, and Penny was making a copy of "The Ride of the Valkyries", just in case something went wrong with the disc.

Mum put the phone down and called for everyone to come to the kitchen. "I need to go over the plans for tonight," she said. "I need to know when we are meeting you and who is staying with whom. Carla, you're staying over at Sophie's, right?"

Carla nodded. That was her alibi. Dad must have had a word with her, because Mum didn't mention Carla's blotched, swollen face.

"And Woody is staying with Ern."

"And I'm staying with Isla," said Penny.

Mum paused. "That's the first I've heard of it," she said.

Penny rolled her eyes. "Mu-um, it's arranged. Isla and Isla's mum are meeting us back at the parade after the carnival is finished."

"No," said Mum. "I don't know her mum. I'm not letting you go off with strangers."

"Isla is NOT strangers," thundered Penny.

"We'll meet you back at Broadway. We'll be there to collect you when you arrive." Mum set her mouth. "It's not safe for you to be wandering about on your own."

"But you've got tickets for the grandstand," said Carla, who had orchestrated this so she could be sure of knowing where her parents were. "How will you get back to Broadway in time?"

"I'll be there," said Mum grimly. "I'll expect to see ALL of you there before you go off with your friends and their parents. And Penny, you'll come home with me."

"But, Mum. . ." Penny's wail was interrupted by the phone ringing.

"Leave it," said Dad.

"I'm expecting to hear from the caterer – I have to answer it," snapped Mum, rushing out to the hall.

When she had gone Penny thumped the table. "It's not FAIR!" she stormed.

"Sorry," said Dad. "There's so much going on, we haven't had time to arrange all this properly. Try to

understand. We only want to make sure you're safe."
He hesitated. "Maybe I should call Isla's mum to
explain."

"No, no, no," said Carla hurriedly. "It will be fine.
You've got enough to worry about." It wouldn't do for
Dad to speak to Mrs Godfrey only to discover that
Penny hadn't arranged to stay there at all.

Dad frowned. "Even so, it will look rude if I don't. . ."
He looked up as Mum walked in, her face lit up with
excitement.

"It's Maria," she said. "She's gone into labour, and
she's asking for me.

Yes, thought Carla. Yes, yes, yes! She winked at Penny
and grinned.

With Mum out of the way, tonight ought to be much
easier.

At four o'clock, Dad took them to the barn.

Mum had already left, belting down the road in her
little car. "Are you sure you don't mind if I miss
everything?" she'd said anxiously. "Because obviously I
don't know how long it will take, but Maria is my oldest
friend and. . ."

"Go and have a baby," said Carla, smiling. "We
understand."

"I'm so sorry. . ."

"Say hi to Maria for us," said Woody.

Mum had gathered them all in her arms. "You are
such wonderful children. I don't deserve you."

Through the folds of her mother's coat, Penny winked at Carla, and Carla felt a lurch of guilt. They watched their mother hurtle off. Carla's stomach turned over. The next time she would see her mother, it would all be done.

"That's her taken care of for the night," said Penny with satisfaction. "First babies always take ages. Maybe I'll find a way to be at the beach after all."

The Moons entered the barn.

"Wow!" said Dad, looking at *To Valhalla!* "She looks amazing. I had no idea." He smiled at Carla. "Grandpa would have been very proud." Everyone stood back to look at their cart. Grandpa's little boat had been transformed into a carnival spectacle. *Valkyrie* sat on the trailer, her sails unfurled and striped bunting hanging from her rigging. The dragon figurehead loomed up, gleaming gold. The light-frame, now secured to the mast, had been wired into the generator and the bulbs shone red and yellow. Bronze-coloured shields were strung over the sides of the boat, which appeared to be sailing in a sea of painted waves.

The Sparks had already cleared the floor and had opened the big threshing doors, and Mr Blake, Ern's dad, now reversed in. They did a final test of the light bulbs, checked the generator and hitched the trailer to the tractor.

Everything was ready.

Everything, Carla thought, apart from herself. She couldn't stop trembling. There was so much at stake.

The tractor drove away down the road, towing *To Valhalla!* It was going at a fair speed, and the children watched anxiously as their cart bounced over the potholes. Ern waved from the tractor cab.

"Good luck, everyone!" he called.

Carla eyed the large mound covered by the orange tarpaulin in the corner of the barn. Luckily neither Dad nor Mr Blake had been the slightest bit interested in what lay underneath: they'd been too busy with *To Valhalla!*

Penny turned to Carla.

"Shouldn't you be at Sophie's by now?"

Carla looked at her watch. She should have been at her friend's house fifteen minutes ago. "See you later," she said, and everyone gave each other high fives. They were all grinning. "Stay calm," said Carla, "and it will be all right."

"Anyone would think you were going into battle," said Dad, looking amused.

"Oh, we are, Mr Moon, we are," said Bullet solemnly. Then there was a tentative knock on the door and Mrs Sudra came in. Isla's dad arrived shortly after and the Sparks dispersed. Ratsy was going with Bullet, and Samantha was squeezing in with Isla.

"I can walk to Sophie's on my own," said Carla. "It's not far."

"I'm not letting you out on your own in the dark," said Dad indignantly. "Especially not tonight. People go mad on carnival night."

"I'm thirteen," said Carla. She hoped Dad wouldn't

hang around at Sophie's. There was too much work to be done.

"So you keep reminding me," muttered Dad.

Sophie was sitting waiting on her doorstep, wrapped and hooded in her Goth cloak. She watched Carla climb out of Dad's car.

"So," she said, as Dad drove off, "we're really going through with this."

Upstairs in Sophie's black bedroom, Carla passed over the box with the dress inside. "Are you sure you don't mind?"

Sophie tore open the box and shook out the dress. "I've wanted to be Carnival Princess all my life. Let's face it: I'll never get to do it otherwise. I haven't got the looks, and I can't afford plastic surgery. You're my ticket to glory!"

Carla smiled. Everyone would be thinking she was going to be on the carnival cart, waving and simpering with all the other princesses. But she wasn't. She had a decoy. Carla was going to be at the funeral parlour, stealing her grandpa.

"Don't you mind missing the funeral?" asked Carla.

"With respect" – Sophie examined Carla's silver tiara – "I would rather be sitting on cushions, surrounded by adoring fans, in a beautiful dress, being told how wonderful I am, than setting fire to your grandpa on a lonely beach." It was, Carla conceded, a fair point. "You do what you have to do," said Sophie. "I like to think I'm playing my part on the home front."

"Oh, you are," said Carla, grinning.

"It's about drama," said Sophie. "I like dressing up and having people look at me. Goth vampire zombie-girl to princess is a natural progression, if you ask me."

"I'd have thought you'd rather be at the beach," said Carla. "You being into dark stuff and being morbid."

"It's all for show," said Sophie airily. "Give me the sugar pink every time." The blonde wig looked pretty weird on Sophie, but once they'd arranged the tiara and pearls, there was a possibility they'd get away with it.

"Just don't say anything," said Carla, trimming the wig with a pair of nail scissors. "You'll be found out straight away." Shoes were a problem. Sophie's feet were a whole size bigger than Carla's, and they couldn't squeeze her feet into the silver ballet pumps the Carnival Princess committee had provided.

"I feel like Cinderella's ugly sister," moaned Sophie, examining her squashed toes. They decided she should wear her silver Doc Martens instead.

"Say the others didn't fit," said Carla.

"Relax, it'll be fine." Sophie slipped into the dress and Carla zipped it up. Together they arranged the wig and tiara and Carla placed the sash over Sophie's shoulders.

BIGWICH CARNIVAL PRINCESS

"You look amazing," admitted Carla. Sophie arranged the pink-velvet cloak and put up the hood. She gave her black Goth cloak to Carla.

"How do we get into the car without anybody seeing us?" asked Carla. They couldn't get caught at this early stage. But Sophie had a plan. "Family," she shouted, opening her door, "stay out of the way. Carla is coming downstairs and she doesn't want anybody to see her until she's on the carnival float. She's a bit of a prima donna like that."

"Sophie," hissed Carla as they heard bellows of laughter from downstairs, "that wasn't exactly what I meant."

"Same result," said Sophie. She gave herself one last appraisal in the mirror. "If I cross my eyes I look just like you," she said.

Carla put her hood up and crept out of the room. There was no one about.

"It's OK, we're in the kitchen," called Sophie's mum. "You're quite safe, Carla. We don't want to spoil your big moment."

Carla and Sophie raced to the stairs.

"Sophie, why are you wearing Carla's dress?" asked a small voice. It was Elsa, Sophie's three-year-old sister. She was wearing her pyjamas and clutching a large inflatable hammer.

"Because I'm pretending to be her, only it's secret, so don't tell anyone," said Sophie. She winked at Carla, who was horrified. "Don't worry, no one will believe her if she says anything. Whoever believes a three-year-old?"

The car was unlocked. The girls sat in the back, their hoods up. Then Sophie phoned her dad on her mobile to tell him they were ready.

"But why are *you* being all secretive, Sophie?" he asked as he got into the driver's seat, keeping his eyes firmly forward as instructed.

"Solidarity," muttered Sophie. Carla was glad her friend had unusual dress sense. It meant no one raised an eyebrow at the fact that there were two hooded girls in the car. Both girls kept their hoods pulled low over their faces all the way to the carnival office. Sophie's dad thought it was hilarious.

"We couldn't possibly spoil your grand entrance now, Carla," he chuckled. "I had no idea you were so vain." Then, mercifully, he switched on the radio and fiddled about for the football, so no one had to say anything more until they arrived.

"Should I come in and deliver you to the right person?" he said, pulling over.

"BYE!" Sophie slammed the door and the pair of them raced away into the darkness.

There was no one in reception, but a crowd of people was in the next room. "I feel sick," whispered Sophie. "What if someone spots me? What if my wig falls off?"

"They only know me from the photographs," said Carla. "And I didn't turn up to the rehearsal – I said I was ill. The person to avoid is Mrs Parks. She made the dresses. She shouldn't be here, but if she is, don't look her in the eye. If you get cornered, use this." Carla handed her friend a huge spotted handkerchief. "Just blow your nose." Sophie's bright red mouth twisted into a grin. She looked crazy. "You know, you are beautiful," said Carla. "But you look wonderful without all this stuff too."

"Possibly," said Sophie. "But personally I like all the gaudiness. And this is probably the only opportunity I will have in my life to wear a full-length pink dress, and to sit on a throne in front of thousands of cheering crowds."

Carla nodded, but it sounded like her idea of a nightmare. She gave her friend a quick hug and pushed her in the direction of the carnival room. Sophie turned back, her eyes sparkling. "My dream is about to come true," she said. "I hope yours does too." Then she was gone. Carla couldn't resist peeking through the glass doors for just an instant, to see what happened. She watched as a woman swept down on Sophie, ticked something on a clipboard and ushered her in.

"Aren't you supposed to be in there?" Carla froze. Mrs Parks was just behind her. "It's Carla, isn't it? Why haven't you got the dress on yet?"

"No, I'm Carla's friend," mumbled Carla. Then she fled, cursing herself. She'd nearly ruined everything. She stepped out into the night, the doors swishing behind her.

It had begun.

Carnival

Carla was on her own after dark in the middle of town. Her parents would go mad if they knew. As far as they were concerned, their eldest daughter was safely ensconced in Carnival HQ with the other princesses and the Carnival Queen. Carla put the thought to the back of her mind. She had one full hour before the carnival began – plenty of time to make her way to Broadway. She scooted up the road to the Methodist chapel. The place was open, selling teas and coffees to the people hurrying past, to officials in yellow jackets and to a few masqueraders already dressed in their outfits. Street traders were hawking their wares of glow-bangles, flashing rabbit ears and luminous light-sabres. The chip caravans and burger bars were opening their shutters and lighting the gas. A gang of boys, a little older than she, roamed past chatting and stuffing their mouths with chips. Carla

looked up over the street lights to the moon and stars
above.

"Are you ready, Grandpa?"

She shot into the brightly lit Methodist hall. The walls
were lined with posters advertising jumble sales and
notices asking people to donate money so they could
send a goat to Africa. She crossed the hall and headed
for the ladies'. There she locked herself in the largest
cubicle and opened her bag. Inside she had:

a set of keys to the undertakers'
two mobile telephones
three boxes of matches, two lighters and three
    emergency boxes of firelighters
a torch
a multi-bit screwdriver
a hammer
a neatly coiled three-weave blue nylon rope
a packet of love letters
a Viking costume complete with helmet (with horns)
Grandpa's penknife.

Dad had teased her on the way to Sophie's that
princesses didn't normally carry such large handbags.

"It's all make-up," she'd said.

There was a knock at the door.

"Halloo . . . Is everything all right in there?"

"Fine," said Carla, unlatching the door and coming

out in full regalia. She had transformed herself into a Viking, with helmet and cardboard body armour. She'd decided to leave off the elasticated beard until the last minute.

"Oh, I *see*." A woman with brown curly hair and not much of a chin stood smiling at her. "We have an invasion. Have you come to burn, rape and pillage?"

"Just a bit of burning," muttered Carla, racing past her and out into the night.

It was even busier outside now. Crowds were already gathering, even though the procession wouldn't arrive for at least an hour. Onlookers were staking out their pitches. Most of the flats above the shops had the top windows open, and people were drinking beer and hanging out to watch. Big barricades had been placed on the pavement to keep the crowds off the roads. A tight-knit group of policemen marched past, swinging their arms, truncheons dangling from their belts. A group of lads sat on a roof above her head, drinking from cans and spitting down into the street. Frankly, the place was crazy. Carla understood why her parents were keen that she shouldn't be out on her own.

"Glow stick, darling?" A skinny man in a hooded raincoat waved a rainbow of batons at her.

"No, thanks." She ran off down the street, pushing and weaving through the crowds, heading for Broadway.

Broadway parade was a chaos of noise and

movement. A man in a bright green jacket stood shouting directions through a megaphone, and she guessed about fifty carts of varying sizes were lined up in rows. Masqueraders were having their make-up adjusted or testing their lights. There were pirates, witches, skeletons and cartoon characters.

"Excuse me." Carla was jostled as Tarzan strode by. He wore a chest wig and leopard-skin pants. Carla thought he must be freezing. She fastened her beard over her chin and looked around for *To Valhalla!* One of the carts, *The Lion King*, was testing its sound system, and music from the show blasted out into the night. No one could hear the man with the megaphone any more, so he shouted even louder. People milled all around her, gabbling into mobile phones, queuing for the Portaloos and swigging water from the plastic bottles a drinks company was handing out. Despite the bright lights from the carts, and the street lamps, it was dark and cold. Twisting shadows moved over the ground, and Carla felt a sudden shiver travel down her back. There was so much shouting, so much noise and confusion. She felt small and lonely.

"Hey." Someone grabbed her arm and she instinctively pulled away.

"It's me."

It was Ern. He was dressed in his Viking costume. He was Thor, god of thunder, and wore a sack with neck- and armholes cut out and a red cloth belted round his middle, and big brown lace-up boots. He also had a horned helmet with a large rain cloud attached to it. He carried a papier-mâché thunderbolt.

"I'm wearing my sister's leggings," he admitted. "I know it's not very warlike, but it's November." He grinned at her. "How's it going?"

"You're not supposed to recognize me," said Carla, overwhelmed with relief that she was no longer alone. "I'm in disguise."

"I'd recognize you anywhere," he said. Then he shut his mouth and looked at his boots. Carla felt a hot blush crawl up her cheeks. Neither of them had mentioned The Kiss since it happened.

"Where's the cart?" she finally managed to say.

"Follow me," he said and tentatively held out his hand.

He led her past devils and witches, between masked horsemen and dancing skeletons, and wound around showgirls and majorettes and clowns. Finally, close to the back of the parade, they found *To Valhalla!* Carla smiled; sure, it wasn't as brightly lit as some of the other floats, and compared to, say, *Lion King,* it was tiny. But it looked good. The whole point of carnival was that it was over the top, often tacky, fun, a chance to dance away the cold. But *To Valhalla!* looked almost dignified, even with the red-and-white bulbs flashing in the darkness. *Valkyrie*'s sails gently moved up and down and the bunting fluttered in the breeze. The tractor, to Carla's faint disgust, had an enormous pair of horns attached to the cab.

"Dad secretly made them," explained Ern. "I couldn't say no; I hope that's all right. They're made from Perspex."

Carla thought they were awful and could imagine what Woody would say. "We've got to keep the troops happy," she said faintly. "Are you sure you're OK with driving the tractor later?" she whispered.

Ern shrugged. "I haven't got much choice. It will be fine." Mr Blake was chatting to the driver in the cab of the next tractor. Bullet's mum was hanging around, trying to make Bullet put something on. "Vikings did not wear mittens," Carla heard him protest. She didn't think Bullet's mum would recognize her as they didn't know each other. It was a good job, because she was insisting on walking alongside them the whole way. Everyone seemed to be busy, adjusting the cart, sorting out their costumes, making phone calls. Samantha was already sitting with her oars, doing a few practice strokes.

Carla grinned at everyone and slipped quietly into her place right at the back of the cart where no one would see her. After all, she wasn't supposed to be here. Two of the bulbs just seemed to unscrew themselves and smash on the floor, but Isla had a box of spares. Carla, hiding at the back of the cart, felt her spirits plummet as a drizzle of rain coated her face. If it rained too hard, the boat wouldn't burn and everything would go wrong. Then she froze. Making their way through the crowd were Penny and Woody *with Dad*, heading towards the boat. This was wrong! Ratsy's mum was supposed to be dropping them off. Penny and Woody looked very young and small against all the grotesquely painted adults. Carla ducked to starboard and lowered her chin so that her beard draped over her knees.

"Are you sure I can't walk along beside you?" Dad was saying. "Some of the other parents are."

"NO!" Carla heard Penny explode. "Dad, we'll be fine, we're on the float. There are already too many adults. We've got Mrs Supal and Ern's dad looking after us."

"I won't take my eyes off her," said Woody firmly. "We'll see you at the end."

Carla chewed on her lip. Dad was going to go frantic when two of his children weren't at the designated meeting point. She planned to send him a text at some point, saying they had gone to watch the squibbing. It was a flimsy excuse, but she hoped it would do.

"I'll just take a peek further up the line to see if I can find Carla's princess float," she heard her father say.

Carla held her breath.

"You'll see her when they're parading; don't spoil her moment," said Woody hurriedly. "You'd better go and get your place in the grandstand. I've heard if people are late, the organizers are giving the tickets to other people."

"All right," sighed Dad. "Just look after your sister. Don't let her out of your sight." Carla smiled. Woody was getting almost as good at lying as she was. She watched Dad melt away through the crowds. For just an instant she wanted to call him back and tell him everything. He might just go along with the plan. He could be there with her on the beach at Grandpa's funeral. He could fetch Mum and they'd all be together. She looked at *To Valhalla!*

She couldn't, just couldn't, jeopardize all this work.

Penny clambered in next to her and looked her over.

"You look awful," she said. "Your own mother wouldn't recognize you."

Finally, everyone was in their places. The people milling around seemed to magically disappear. The carts were loaded and the music began to pump out. A horn sounded, and they were off! At least, they were supposed to be. They were at least three-quarters down the line, and there were forty-six carts, thirty walking displays and many, many small trucks and individual masqueraders. Carla pulled her helmet further down her forehead and took up her oars. Isla was standing ahead of the prow, dressed in a flowing white robe. She was representing Freya, the queen of the Viking gods. She was holding on to the dragon's head; it looked like she was worshipping it, but really she was helping to hold it up, as some of the papier mâché had become soggy. Everyone was straining to see what was going on ahead, but they could only make out lights twinkling, and the blaring music of forty carnival carts. The noise was deafening. Then, with a sharp thrill,

Carla saw the cart three places ahead jerk forward. Another few minutes and the marshal waved them off. Everyone grinned at each other and slapped palms (all except Isla, who was too far away, and Bullet, who was Odin, king of the gods, and was sitting on a throne right at the back of the trailer, next to the generator). Carla wondered what the crowd would make of them, a gang of straggly children dressed up as Viking gods and warriors, rowing a small boat through the streets of Bigwich. No matter, it was carnival. The crowds appeared almost immediately. Thousands of people lined the streets, clapping, cheering or just silently watching. The lights twinkled and the children rowed. Their music was playing through Grandpa's old speakers, but they could barely hear it, as *The Lion King* music drowned everything out. *The Lion King* was so bright, and so huge, the Sparks could see the crowd were drawn to it, rather than to their *To Valhalla!* Carla was pleased about this, the others less so.

"They're using the same costumes the Crusaders had two years ago," hissed Ratsy. "Sharon Macey's sister bought them all off eBay."

"And some of them are TOO FAT to wear them," said Samantha. "Look."

The last masquerader on the the *Lion King* float was a tall, wide man, dressed as a zebra in a skintight black-and-white striped outfit. He had a very large bottom which was wobbling around, flicking his tail and making the Vikings giggle.

Carla's stomach had been churning whilst they were all hanging around, waiting to begin, but now they were off, slowly crawling along the dark streets, she felt calm and detached.

"I'm going to do this, Grandpa," she whispered. "Just watch me go."

She couldn't join in with the chat, though she knew everyone was watching her every move, waiting for directions. She looked at her watch. The entire parade took roughly two hours from start to finish, and in about forty-five minutes they should arrive at Coronation Row. This drag was notorious for hold-ups. Every year masqueraders had to wait for agonizing minutes whilst the whole thing inexplicably came to a halt and no one ever seemed to know why. Some of the stops were so long that even the most energetic performers stopped dancing. But it was a chance to have a drink of water and peer into the crowds, to see if there were any familiar faces. Carla was counting on a Coronation Row hold-up.

Carla checked her watch. Five to eight. So far there had only been one five-minute stop, but they hadn't been anywhere close to where she needed to be. She was depending on one of the long hold-ups so she and Woody could abandon ship.

"Shouldn't we have got off by now?" asked Woody. He wiped his nose on his sleeve. Ern caught her eye. He'd wanted to jump off with them, but, as Carla pointed out, his dad would be pretty suspicious if he went missing in the middle of the parade.

Eight-thirty and still no decent hold-up. Carla's stomach was churning with nerves. They were on Coronation Row. She wondered how Sophie was getting on. She hoped the wind hadn't blown her wig off. She noticed a gang of older lads sitting on the barriers, calling and jeering. Further up the boat, Woody saw them and froze. Then he put down his oars, pulled his beard well over his face and climbed over everyone to the back of the cart. Carla watched bemused as he picked up the fire bucket full of water. Suddenly, when he was level with the lads, he let out a roar and chucked the water over the head of the nearest.

"WHO'S WET HIMSELF NOW, MIKEY DOBBS?" he roared. Carla held her breath. Was this roaring Viking really her shy little brother? The boy fell off the barrier and got up, astonished, water dripping off him.

"That was high risk," remarked Carla, as they moved on and the boy was lost in the crowds.

"It was worth it," said Woody, clambering back into place.

Nine p.m. Carla was sweating. They'd been parading now for ages, the crowd cheering and clapping and the music playing. But carnival *never* went smoothly. Carla was relying on it. But they'd already gone through Coronation Row. She was beginning to think they would never stop. Woody evidently thought so too.

"Shall we just jump off?" he said. "It's going so slow, I'm sure we'll be fine."

"No," said Carla firmly. She'd heard horror stories of people getting their costumes caught in trailer wheels. She wasn't going to put her brother in danger. Nothing was that important. They just had to hold their nerve.

"You shouldn't be here," shouted down Bullet.

Carla ignored him. She didn't want to discuss her plans with the whole of Bigwich.

"Delay up ahead," called Isla from her vantage point at the front. "All the brake lights are coming on."

Carla grabbed Ern's hand without really noticing. "Ouch," he said softly – she'd been digging her nails into his skin. The tractor braked and the trailer came to a halt.

"Now," Carla said, and she and Woody ducked behind the speakers, climbed over the generator and lowered themselves over the stern of the boat to the trailer, then to the ground. They had to get off the side where Mrs Sudra *wasn't*, which meant they had to cross the street, ducking behind the cart to get to the right side of the road.

"Good luck," called Penny, appearing to starboard. "See you later. Oh," she added. "You'd better run, there's a steward coming." Carla clambered over the crowd barriers and watched as Woody was lifted over by a burly man selling whistles.

"Abandoning ship?" he said, grinning. The children disappeared into the crowd. Carla held tightly to Woody's hand as they wound through the bystanders. They stumbled into a group of people in skeleton outfits, the bones glowing in the dark. When they saw Carla and Woody, they all stared through black eyes. Carla felt her neck burn as she picked her way through them.

"*Just put your head down and get on,*" Grandpa advised.

"You don't have to hold my hand," said Woody, trying to pull away.

"Yes, I do," said Carla. They fought to the back of the crowd, squeezing past old men and babies in pushchairs. Carla passed a girl in her class but she wasn't recognized; her beard and helmet were doing their job.

"Look," said Woody, pointing. "*To Valhalla!*"

The children watched their cart crawl past. The stop hadn't been long and Carla was glad they'd been speedy. Their cart looked magical, with the bulbs strung overhead, the sails billowing and the Viking gods and warriors rowing through the air. And she hadn't noticed before, but Ern's dad, driving the tractor, was wearing one of Ratsy's cow-horn helmets.

Suddenly he turned his head and looked straight at her.

"Down!" Carla dragged Woody to the ground. After a minute they ran along the back of the pavement, eventually breaking free of the crowd. They turned into Salt Row. It was a dark, narrow street with tall old buildings and a few flickering street lights. Some of the doors and windows of the houses were boarded up. It was only a step away from all the brightness and action, but here it was totally different. Carla imagined eyes watching her from every window, but she firmly told herself everyone would be at the carnival. In the distance at the other end of Salt Row the front of the parade was passing.

"Look," whispered Woody. "It's the royal float."

Carla knew they didn't have much time, but she couldn't resist going just a little closer.

"Look," she said as she glimpsed a dancing figure in a long pink dress and flying blonde hair, standing on a throne and punching her fists into the air. Then the cart rolled past.

"Was that Sophie?" asked Woody in disbelief. Carla nodded, temporarily lost for words. The children doubled back and turned up the narrow, cobbled dead end leading to the funeral parlour.

"Will the tractor and trailer get up here?" asked Woody.

"Of course it will," snapped Carla. "The hearses do. And you can take your moustache off now."

"It's keeping my mouth warm," said Woody, stroking it. Two sleek hearses sat silently in the courtyard, gleaming in the street light. Carla shivered. One of them was meant for Grandpa. The carnival music bounced off the high walls and into their ears, sounding creepy and distorted. Carla got the key out of her pouch.

"Hurry up, I'm cold," whispered Woody, his eyes shining in the darkness.

"It's even colder in there," muttered Carla, fitting the key in the lock. The door clicked open. Now she had to get to the keypad before the alarm went off. She raced into reception, switching on her torch and keeping the beam low to the ground. She pushed open the door to the prep room and a waft of something strong, like alcohol, greeted her. She headed straight for the alarm pad and lifted it up. There was a green flashing light. She paused.

"I don't like it in here," said Woody.

"Shh!" She was sure that when Rowan had punched in the number the light had been red. She shone the torch on the instructions and sure enough, in bold writing, it said:

RED LIGHT: ALARM SET.
GREEN LIGHT: ALARM DEACTIVATED.

It was already deactivated. But why? Carla decided not to worry. "Follow me," she whispered, and raced back out into the corridor and into the coffin room. She took a chance and switched on the light. Woody grabbed her arm as the strip light blinked into life, illuminating identical wooden coffins standing against the walls.

"It's only a pile of wood," said Carla reassuringly. "Help

me get one on this trolley." Gingerly the children manoeuvred the nearest coffin over the carpet. They had to walk it along, one corner at a time.

"Won't Mr Salt notice it's missing?" asked Woody, whipping his foot away to avoid being crushed by a corner of the coffin.

"No," said Carla firmly. She didn't imagine he came in here and counted them. And if there was one less than he expected, he would hardly think someone had stolen one.

They attempted to lift the coffin on to the trolley. It took all Carla's strength to hold up her end, and she felt her fingers sliding off the wood. "I'm going to drop it," she yelled as it crashed to the floor. "Why do they make them so heavy?" she moaned.

"To make sure no one can get out," said Woody darkly. They tried again, and this time managed to lift the coffin on to the trolley.

"How are we going to lift it once it's got the sandbags in it?" asked Woody.

"We'll manage," said Carla, through gritted teeth. "And there's a hydraulic lifting trolley next door that we can use for Grandpa."

The children wheeled the empty coffin out of the room and through to reception. Carla produced the screwdriver from her bag, clicked in a different head and unscrewed the coffin lid.

They left the empty coffin standing on the cobbles outside.

"What if someone notices?" asked Woody.

"They'll be used to it round here," said Carla. She checked her watch.

Nine forty-five.

How could it be this time already? Fairly soon *To Valhalla!* would pass the grandstand, the official end of the carnival, where Dad, and possibly even Mum, were waiting. Would they notice Woody was missing? Carla hoped not. Most of the Sparks were well disguised, and Carla had instructed Penny to stand right at the front so she *could* be recognized.

"Come on, back to the prep room," said Carla. "Grandpa's waiting."

Stealing Grandpa

Carla didn't dare risk switching on the lights – they'd show through the frosted glass. Instead she wedged her torch under a book. Gloomy shadows shifted and changed shape as the children moved.

"What is this place?" asked Woody in a small voice, looking at the stainless-steel surfaces, and the white tiles on the walls going all the way up to the ceiling. "It looks like the school kitchens."

"This is the prep room, where Mr Salt sorts everyone out," said Carla breezily. She crossed the room to the fridge. "Now, don't be scared," she said. "It's only Grandpa in here." Woody gulped. "Wheel that over." Carla pointed to the large hydraulic trolley. Her tummy was whizzing around like a washing machine and her palms were damp. She didn't want to stop and think about what they were doing. Carla twisted the handle and the huge refrigerator doors swung open. Woody let out a little moan.

"I thought you said only Grandpa was in there," he said shakily.

Six coffins were stacked up on runners in the fridge.

"It must be the cold snap we've had," said Carla. Mercifully, the coffins all had their lids on them. She had to do this properly. All these people in here were special and important to other families. These were other people's loved ones. She mustn't mess this up.

"Carla," said Woody in a small voice. "I don't think I can do this." Carla froze. Slowly she turned her head to look at her brother. He looked scared but this was no time to be merciful.

"Yes you can," she said, "or it'll be you in that fridge." There was silence.

"All right, which one is Grandpa?" sighed Woody, shivering. His name was on one of the middle coffins: "Magnus Michael Hughes". Now Carla was shivering. She really, really didn't like thinking of Grandpa shut in that box.

"Sometimes it's best not to think," said Grandpa. *"Just switch over to automatic pilot."*

"Over here," she ordered, and Woody pushed the lifting trolley up to the fridge. Carla read the operating instructions on the side.

DEPRESS LEVER TO LOWER MAINBED

But she didn't want to lower it; she wanted to make it higher. She figured she needed to do the opposite.

Carla pulled the handle towards her. Nothing happened. She felt a surge of panic. Why wasn't it working? They'd never be able to lift Grandpa down on their own.

"Plug it in?" said Woody, holding a coiled electric flex.

"Go on then," said Carla testily. She was trying not to read the names on the labels on the other coffins, but couldn't help it.

Valerie Grey.

Not Mrs Grey? That was the name of Carla's form teacher. She was sure her first name was Valerie. Could she have died over the half-term? Who would take the register? She had seemed well enough the last time Carla had seen her. She was in fine form, yelling at Nadja Hussman for forgetting her homework. Or was Mrs Grey's first name Ivy?

"Carla" – Woody interrupted her thoughts – "I think it will work now." They manoeuvred the platform up to Grandpa, then smoothly slid his coffin on its runners right on to the lifting platform. It was simple to lower it after that . Everything seemed to slot and click into place. Carla bit her lip. She was fizzing with adrenalin. She closed the door on the fridge (trying hard not to read the remaining names, but who was *Denzel Lyons*?)

Woody busied himself plugging an extension lead into Grandpa's trolley and wheeling it over to the doors.

A loud engine revved outside. "Ern's here," whispered Woody, peering through the frosted glass. Carla unbolted the prep-room door and looked out into the night. Ern was reversing *To Valhalla!* down the alleyway. He stopped just before the courtyard in front of the hearses and switched off the engine. He was alone. Carla scanned the nearby windows. People might wonder why a tractor and carnival float were reversing into a funeral director's courtyard.

"Ready?" called Ern in a low voice. He was still in his Thor costume, minus the helmet. Carla grinned and gave him a thumbs up. Woody wheeled Grandpa out into the courtyard and operated the lever, lifting him up to the level of the trailer, then further up, until he was level with *Valkyrie*'s gunwale. The children pulled out the runner from the trolley and heaved and grunted as Grandpa's coffin finally slid on board.

"You're a Viking now, Grandpa," whispered Carla, hardly daring to believe that everything was going so well. Ern lifted the thwarts from their shelves, shoved the coffin into position and lashed it down with ropes and webbing, securing it to the safety harness at the bottom of the boat.

Woody and Carla sped back into the building with the trolley and reappeared wheeling the empty coffin over the cobbles. Ern didn't waste any time unloading five sandbags into it. One bag slipped through his hands, spilling some of its contents. Carla scrabbled the sand back in its sack.

The children moved the sandbags around so the heaviest end was where the top of Grandpa's body should be, and they placed just one in the leg area. They wedged the bags in tightly, packing them with cardboard from the trailer so they wouldn't slip around, and heaved on the lid, wriggling it until it fitted into position.

"This must be too heavy," puffed Woody. "How do you know it's the right weight?"

"Just get on with it," snapped Carla. There wasn't time to explain that each sandbag weighed fifteen kilos, and the average weight of an adult was seventy kilos, therefore she had five sandbags to go in the coffin. Carla was getting hot. There was so much to do.

"Just keep going, one step at a time, and don't panic," Grandpa advised.

"Right," said Carla as she and Woody pushed the trolley over the cobbles back to the prep room. "Now we have a fake Grandpa."

It was simple but time-consuming to drive fifteen or so screws into place. The first two screws had gone down too deep, but she didn't think that would be a problem.

Carla took Grandpa's name label from her pocket and stuck it in the correct position on the fake. Then she crossed the room and flung open the fridge door.

"Hurry," she urged Woody as he brought the coffin over. "Or we'll miss the tide." She was shaking now and had to keep telling herself that her plan was working, they were going to make it.

The children were leaving the building, and Carla was looking in her pocket for the key, when a window just above them flew open and a head stuck out.

"Hey! What are you doing?"

A Kind of Magic

Someone, somewhere in the building, was thumping downstairs. Carla and Woody stepped back as two men burst into the prep room. One was Rowan and the other, Carla saw with a mixture of horror and relief, was Gus.

"I don't believe this," said Gus, taking in the boat and the tractor outside. He turned to Carla. "You lunatic."

She should have thought of it. Rowan's flat above the undertakers' would most likely have a great view of the carnival. Gus was Rowan's mate, so of course he'd be watching the parade from here. The loud music from the floats would have drowned out the children's noise. But now, in the lull between the end of the parade and the beginning of the fireworks, they must have been overheard.

Rowan looked stricken. "How did they get in? Have they actually. . .?" He peered out into the courtyard.

"What are you doing?" asked Gus.

"Just visiting," said Carla, slamming the door in his face and turning the key. "Drive!" she screamed, leaping on the trailer and dragging Woody after her. They watched the doors shudder as Gus and Rowan pummelled them from inside. Ern drove them out of the courtyard, over the cobbles and into the street.

"Go faster!" shouted Carla, not caring who else they disturbed.

"Not easy!" yelled back Ern. "This is a narrow space."

Carla wanted to scream with tension. She knew the door wouldn't hold for ever; besides, Rowan lived here, he would have his own key. It might be in his pocket. "Go, go, go!" she urged as Ern drove them into the street. But then they weren't going anywhere. "What is it?" she screeched. "Turn left, then left again and we'll be on the ring road. Go."

"He can't," said Woody. "We're in a one-way street. He'd be breaking the law."

Carla looked at him incredulously. "Who cares about the law? Look what we're doing!"

"Someone might come the other way," called Ern. "There could be an accident." Carla groaned. She hadn't realized the road was one way when she'd planned the route on the map.

"*Try not to make a bad situation worse,*" whispered Grandpa.

The boys were right. So she only had one choice. "Turn back to Coronation Row," she said. It wouldn't work, they would get caught, but it was either that or wait here for Rowan and Gus.

"*If you get a chance, take it,*" said Grandpa. "*Chances are a kind of magic.*"

"You want us to rejoin the carnival?" called Ern.

"Yes," said Carla.

"You're crazy," said Woody as they lurched forward. Carla held her breath as they left the quiet street and reached the busy junction. Crowd barriers blocked their path, but a gang of laughing teenagers pulled them out of the way to let the tractor pass.

"We got lost," shouted Woody. "Thanks!" They pulled into the road and the crowd cheered. They were right at the end of the parade, some distance behind the last cart in the procession, *Waterworld*, which was playing loud samples of whales singing and featured dancing men in fish tails.

Carla crouched by Grandpa's coffin. "They're cheering you off, Grandpa," she whispered. Behind the float, a little way back, she saw a glow of orange-and-yellow flames and sparkles. The walking fireworks were coming. Then she saw Isla and Samantha in the crowd, still in costume, gazing at them in astonishment.

"Jump on," she called. Ern slowed so the girls could scramble over the crowd barriers and up on to the boat. They immediately took up their positions at the oars.

"Oh no, is that him?" Samantha blurted out, edging away from the coffin.

"Yup," said Carla, grinning. "Don't worry, he won't

bite." There was no sign of Gus and Rowan. Not yet. Did they know she had Grandpa? If they looked in the fridge, they'd find the fake coffin in the right place with his name on. They might not bother to follow the children at all.

To Valhalla! crawled along the road, and the remaining Vikings waved at the people on the pavements. The crowds had thinned and most of the small children had gone. All at once a steward was running up to them, and shouting through a megaphone.

"Entry '*To Valhalla!*', you can't do the carnival *twice* . . . you are disqualified."

"We got confused," shouted Woody. "Sorry."

"The board will discuss your permanent exclusion from carnival after this!" the steward thundered.

"It won't happen," muttered Isla. "That's *Safety Dave*. He's the carnival-committee member in charge of health and safety. No one likes him. If we're disqualified, we'll just change our name."

"Let them stay," shouted someone in the crowd. Then another voice called, "A TROPHY FOR *TO VALHALLA!*"

"THEY'RE ONLY KIDS." All at once the whole crowd was roaring support and clapping and booing Safety Dave.

"Where is your Responsible Person?" spluttered Safety Dave. He looked over at Ern. "Who's that driving in there?"

"We're so sorry. We didn't mean this to happen." Carla pretended to wipe away a tear.

"Move on, the squibbers are coming," roared someone in the crowd.

"But. . ." Dave looked at the advancing lights.

"MOVE," roared the crowd.

"Go on then. You're a fire risk if you stay here. I'll deal with you later." Safety Dave stood back and furiously waved them on. Carla clutched her oar, turning hot and cold with nerves.

"Just keep rowing," Woody advised.

Carla looked at her watch. They were running late. If they missed the tide, how would they get *Valkyrie* over the mud to the water? She gritted her teeth.

Now only twenty or so metres behind *To Valhalla!*, rows and rows of men and women marched with sparklers and whirring flames dancing above their heads. They held whizzing fireworks up high on big sticks. There were fire jugglers and spinners. Women in gold catsuits danced and a man with hair down to his feet breathed out a cloud of flame.

"Grandpa would have loved this," said Woody. "Even if it all goes wrong, Carla, this is a good send-off." Carla nodded. She hadn't given up yet. They were rounding the corner into Canal Street when there was a loud bang and Woody nearly fell off the trailer in alarm. A shower of red-and-green sparks filled the sky. Another firework exploded into the air and they were driving through golden rain.

"This is brilliant," shouted Woody. Then, just as they passed the roundabout at the bottom of the exchange,

Ern turned into a side street where there were no barriers blocking the road. He drove a little way and stopped. The tractor engine went dead. Carla heard the River Wich flowing nearby.

"Ern. . ." began Carla. "The next right would be better. . ."

Ern stood up in the tractor seat. "We're not going anywhere," he said, his gaze fixed on Carla's face. "We're out of gas." Carla's mind started whirring. Where was the nearest garage? Who should she send for a can of diesel? She looked hopefully at a gap in the buildings. Beyond this was the river. If there was a way they could get the boat on to the river, they could row Grandpa to the sea.

"You can't take the boat down the river, it's too dangerous," said Ern, reading her thoughts. He'd slipped out of the cab to stand alongside her. It felt nice to have someone by her side. She knew he was right. Grandpa would be horrified to think of them going down the deep, fast, treacherous River Wich. Carla knew Woody would want to go with her, and she couldn't risk it. It wouldn't be fair to Mum. But what now? Was there time to get diesel from somewhere? What garage would sell it to a kid? At least no one was paying them any attention. The spectators had their backs to them, observing the squibbing display.

Then, with a jolt, Carla saw Gus breaking out of the crowds and heading towards them.

They were finished.

"Hello."

Carla watched numbly as Gus climbed up on to the cart and into the boat, making the light-frame wobble and leaving dirty boot marks on the wooden waves. He sat on the locker in the stern of the boat and stretched out his long legs. He drummed his fingers on the coffin.

"Get off," said Carla weakly. "This is our cart. You've got no right to be here."

"Actually, no," said Gus. "I've got more right than you to be here. You see, Magnus left me *Valkyrie*."

"What?"

"He left me a letter. He said he'd leave me *Valkyrie*. We used to go out sailing together. Mostly before you lot came along, that is," he added.

"So what do you want?" Carla asked weakly.

"I want to know why there appears to be a coffin on my boat. I want to know why you kids broke into the funeral parlour."

"It's just part of the cart," said Carla. "Valhalla is the resting place of the Vikings. A coffin makes it more authentic."

"Don't lie to me, Carla; I know you've got Magnus in there."

Carla felt her spirits plummet. How did he know? How?

"In the letter, Magnus mentioned a Viking funeral," said Gus, examining a shield. Carla gaped at him. "I know it was his last wish."

"So are you going to help?" asked Carla incredulously.

"You're not burning this little boat of mine," said Gus. "Not in a million years." Carla listened to the river. It seemed to be getting louder. Maybe there was a bore coming, when a wall of water piled down the river at high tide. But it couldn't be high tide already, could it? The remaining Sparks stared at her, waiting for her to do something. But she felt paralysed. She couldn't move. But as Gus slipped off the boat to the pavement her mind began racing again. She fingered the burn on her wrist. Maybe she could somehow get *Valkyrie* to the river after all. They could send Gus for fuel, and when he was gone they'd drag the trailer to the river wall. But then what? Carla noticed a large dark car quietly part through the crowds. To her amazement the crowd let it through and turned back to watch the parade. She realized she was looking at a hearse.

"Are you going to take him back?" said Woody sadly.

"I repeat, I'm not going to let you burn MY boat," said Gus, waving at the hearse. He turned to Carla. "You'll have to burn another one." Carla looked at him. She didn't understand him; she never had.

"I think the *Julie* would be more appropriate," Gus went on. The hearse pulled in behind the trailer and Rowan got out. He was wearing a top hat and was dressed from head to toe in black.

"Quickly," he said. "There's a topless fire-juggling woman going past. We have about three minutes of relative obscurity."

Carla looked at them. Could this mean they were on

her side? Surely not? Gus hated them. They hated Gus. It was the way things were.

"But what are you going to do with him?" she blurted as Rowan undid the tailgate and Gus started slicing through the webbing securing the coffin with a wicked-looking knife. "Where are you going to take him?"

"To the sea, of course," said Gus. "We have twenty minutes before high tide, then another twenty of slack water." He shook his head at her. "It might still work, you mad girl. But I need your Viking friends to help move him."

Carla could only watch, dumbfounded, as Woody, Ern, Isla and Samantha helped Rowan and Gus lift the coffin over the side of *Valkyrie*. Then they slid it along the trailer and gently unloaded it from the back and into the hearse.

"I don't believe you're going to help us," said Carla, not lifting a finger.

"He was my grandpa too," panted Gus. "Not in blood, I know. But in everything else." Carla watched as they shut the back of the hearse. "Anyone see us?" asked Gus, looking over at the crowds.

Rowan shrugged. "I don't think so. I had a hard job driving away from the firewoman myself. She's quite impressive."

Carla was still not convinced they were going to help.

"Your brother is a lazy so-and-so," explained Rowan, holding out a hand to help her off *Valkyrie*. "He wouldn't have done this on his own. You had to do all the work. Now he can come in at the end and steal all your glory."

"*Chances,*" Grandpa reminded Carla, "*are like magic.*"

Carla allowed Rowan to help her down. He set her on the pavement and opened the passenger door of the hearse. "Come on, we've got a sea to catch."

Carla looked up at Ern.

He grinned. "Go for it."

High Tide

Carla and Woody perched on the slippery back seat. The inside of the car was very clean and smelled strongly of polish. Carla couldn't shake the suspicion that Gus and Rowan were taking them to the police station or straight to Dad. But they were going in the right direction. She had no idea a hearse could go so fast. And she had to admit, it had its uses. It should have been impossible to drive through town on carnival night. But not, it seemed, if you were in a hearse. Everyone was going out of their way to let them through. Woody had collected the life jackets, the rope and some of the tools from *Valkyrie* and had put them in the boot. Thank goodness for Woody, thought Carla. She would have forgotten.

Ern, Isla and Samantha had stayed with the tractor and *Valkyrie*. Ern was going to phone and get his mate to buy some diesel from the twenty-four-hour garage and then drive back to Broadway.

"But how are we going to get *Julie* to the sea?" piped up Carla. It was weird not being in control any more, though she had to admit things seemed to be running a lot more smoothly now Gus and Rowan had stepped in. "Are we going to row her?" she asked, having visions of them rowing down the river in the dead of night, scaring all the eel poachers.

"You're crazy," said Gus. "But I'm not. We'd drown."

Carla wondered if Gus had known all along what they had been doing, even when he'd turned up at the shore and rescued them from the helicopters.

"*Julie* is already on a boat trailer, isn't she? So this old bus will just haul her to the sea instead," said Gus. Carla thought about this. Maybe *Julie* was a better choice than *Valkyrie*; she'd been Grandpa's boat for years and years.

"You know who she's named after, don't you?" asked Gus. "Julie is the woman Magnus really loved. He knew her before your grandma, but he was on shore leave and had a fling. He was going to go back to Julie, but then your grandma fell pregnant with your mum, so he married her instead." Carla looked out of the window. All this sounded very grown-up and not really her business. But it fitted with the stuff in Grandpa's letters.

Little Wichley was in darkness. Carla guessed the villagers would be in bed or at the carnival. Rowan reversed the hearse down the side lane to Grandpa's barn. Then everyone had to help haul out *Julie* on her trailer. Carla put her cheek on *Julie*'s still-damp hull and inhaled her smell of sour wood. Then she had to push with every ounce of strength. "Ow!" screeched Gus, sucking his fingers. He'd pinched them as he hooked the trailer on to the hearse's tow bar. Carla smiled. Gus was still Gus. Next they had to pull the mast and the sprit from a stack of poles resting in one corner. Carla and Woody heaved out the sails from under Grandpa's couch. They were brown with age and smelled rotten.

"Are you sure this will work?" Rowan asked as Gus unhooked a coil of rope from a nail on the wall.

"I have no idea," said Gus. "But these types of boats are easy to rig, though not so easy to sail." Carla had no idea that Gus knew so much about sailing and boats. She kept checking the time. She was sure they were going to miss the tide, though they'd gained some extra minutes because the hearse was so much faster than the tractor would have been. She wondered what lies Penny was spinning to Dad to keep him happy.

Gus and Rowan lifted the heavy old sea chains from their hooks on the wall and Carla helped to drag them on to the trailer. Everyone was back in the hearse and Rowan was pulling out into the road when Carla shouted, "Stop!" She opened her door. "I forgot something. Come on, Woody. I'll need your help." A few minutes later she and Woody hauled Napoleon out of the barn. Carla's hands felt sticky after touching him and some of his fur had come away in her fingers.

Gus helped them to load him into the boat. "Is he going to read the service?" He strapped him down.

"He's going to Valhalla with Grandpa," said Carla, daring him to disagree.

Finally they were speeding along the dark lanes, *Julie* bouncing along behind on the trailer. Gus and Rowan were busy talking about the tide and the wind and how long it would take for *Julie* to sink. Then they fired questions at Carla about ropes and firelighters and her other preparations at the beach.

Woody coughed. "Um. . ."

"What is it?" Carla asked.

"What about Mum?"

"Haven't you thought of her before now?" asked Gus. "Did you say you'd stashed plenty of paraffin at the beach?"

"I wonder if there's a way of including her," murmured Woody.

Gus passed his mobile phone to Carla. "Ring her," he said offhandedly. "Tell her to meet us at the beach in half an hour."

"Go on," whispered Woody. "It'll be all right, you'll see."

Carla hesitated, then punched in her mother's mobile number, but her finger hovered over the call button. She gave Gus back his phone. "She's attending a birth," she said. "I'd better not."

It was dark at the beach. The wind blustered over the sand dunes and the waves raced in. Carla shrank in the cold. She felt detached from the others. They'd parked by the sand dunes and loaded Grandpa's coffin on to *Julie*. It was just about manageable with Gus and Rowan, but Grandpa was still very heavy. Carla heaved with every bit of strength in her body to get him into the boat. It was a good job Grandpa wasn't a giant, otherwise they'd never have managed. When he was on board, everyone helped to drag the trailer through the gap in the dunes. Then they slid *Julie* down from the trailer and she sat beached just below the high tide line. Gus, Rowan and Woody erected the mast, slotting it into place and attaching the sprit sail.

"No snotter," yelled Gus, ferreting through a pile of old ropes. "We'll have to improvise. Hold this torch." Carla blinked. This was a side of Gus she had never seen, though he was as unpleasant as ever, calling her and Woody "brats" and trying to order them around. She shook herself and squelched through the mud to help pull out the sails, in places so damp they'd almost fused together. They soaked them in paraffin, then attached them to the mast. Everything seemed to take ages and the water was washing over her feet before the sails were in place, but they billowed out nicely and Carla drew in her breath. This was fantastic! She hardly dared to believe that it was actually going to work. They were so close!

Gus and Rowan spoke in quiet voices, passing each other ropes and breaking open box after box of firelighters and arranging them in a jumble of flickering torchlight. Then the moon came out from behind a cloud and the sea lit up, sparkling silver grey. Dark clouds scudded overhead. Carla looked up and blinked as a cloud seemed to take on the face of Grandpa. Yes, it was Grandpa, and he was smiling. She tugged at Woody's sleeve.

"Look," she said. "Look at that." Woody looked and she knew he'd seen him too. Then the winds blew, the clouds moved and Grandpa vanished. "Magic again," whispered Carla. Now she'd seen him she felt happy and exhilarated. She'd ditched her wig and helmet in the hearse and was wearing the home-made trousers, her thin dark top, her sacking tunic and boots. The wind whipped through her, sending her hair flying around her face and cutting through her clothes, sending goosebumps all up her arms and legs. It was an offshore wind, though, perfect for launching Grandpa, so she didn't mind. She watched as Rowan and Gus secured Grandpa's coffin to *Julie,* lashing him down with thick coils of rope and weighting him with his sea chains. She and Woody had pushed both of Barney's mud horses over to *Julie,* and Rowan lifted them on the boat to lie either side of Grandpa's coffin. They'd float them out, then ski back to shore with them.

"So what does her ladyship wish me to do with the manky old bear?" asked Gus. "Only there's a load of rope falling out of the hole in his leg."

"Put him in the boat," said Carla. She looked out to sea. The water was racing up the beach over the shining mud. She shivered, remembering how she had fallen into the mud hole. She hoped the mud horses would slide them safely back to shore. But it was risky.

She looked at Napoleon, and stared at the old rope curling out where his back paw should have been.

"Don't go putting yourself or anyone else at risk."

"We need a line," she said. "We need a line to guide us back to shore. Woody, quick." She and Woody pulled the rope out from Napoleon's foot. It went on and on, like a conjuring trick. Napoleon was literally stuffed with it. It was about fifteen metres long and seemed strong. Carla ran with one end back over the beach to the concrete war platform. She wound the rope round and round a thick pillar and fastened it tightly. Then she sped back to the boat, where Rowan and Gus were still cramming firelighters in every nook and cranny.

"Look at the water," said Rowan. The waves were no longer travelling up over the beach but just lapped on the mud. The sea was huge and full, and the lights of Wales seemed a long, long way away. According to Carla's watch, this was slack water. They had to launch *Julie* now, so she caught the outgoing current before they were left standing in a field of mud. Out here, once the tide turned, it raced swiftly back out to sea, and the breezy headwind should help propel *Julie* with it. "Come on," she said, taking charge. "Let's do it."

Rowan and Gus each sloshed four more cans of paraffin over the boat and coffin and bear and all up the mast, and the air was briefly filled with a pungent sharp smell before the wind whipped it away. Rowan tied another thick rope to *Julie*'s stern and coiled the other end round his arm.

"We nearly forgot these," said Woody, leaning in and tucking the bundle of letters under the coffin

"Now we get wet," called Gus. "Stay out of the water, you two rats." But Carla couldn't stay ashore. She put her cheek to *Julie*'s stern and together all four of them heaved her over the slippery mud and into deeper water. The freezing sea crept over her feet, then up over her ankles. Woody stood next to her, his teeth chattering as he pushed. Their feet sank into the mud beneath the water, making it hard to walk. Rowan and Gus pushed from the back. They were pushing for ages and Carla thought they weren't getting anywhere. She couldn't get a grip in the mud and the water was too shallow. They'd never launch her. But then a wave broke over her knees and with a big shove *Julie* was floating. There was a strong gust of wind. She listed strongly to one side and Carla worried she was going to tip right over.

"Help me get on," said Gus, and together everyone heaved him into the boat and held *Julie* steady as he slotted the daggerboard into place. This should balance her and stop her tipping over. Now that she was more stable in the water, she started pulling forward as the wind caught her sails. Carla watched as Gus shipped the rudder and tied the tiller so that *Julie* would steer in one direction, hopefully out to sea. Then Gus slipped over the side and into the water.

Quarter past midnight.

Carla's feet were numb. She had never felt so cold in

her life, but she waded deeper and deeper into the dark sea, the end of Napoleon's rope tucked under her arm. She could feel the currents sucking at her, dragging her in. After a few minutes they didn't need to push, but gently guided *Julie* out, feeling her pull with the wind. Carla felt a shot of alarm as she felt herself sinking and grabbed the sides of the boat to stay upright. Looking over, she saw that Woody was doing the same.

"No further," ordered Gus now the water was up to their thighs and *Julie* was straining at the rope attached to the stern. They pulled the mud horses from the boat which bobbed about in the waves before they sank. Carla splashed round the boat to put them the right way up. She pulled her feet out of the mud to find the narrow wooden platform. Woody joined her, standing on the strip of slowly sinking wood. Then Gus lighted a taper; he slipped a jar over the flame to stop the wind blowing it out.

"Quick, quick," he shouted. "Who's going to throw the first flame? One of you crazies?"

Carla rinsed her hands in the sea because they stank of paraffin, then took the taper from Gus. Her hands were shaking and she thought the tide might pull her right under the boat. She was in danger now, deadly, deep danger.

"Do it now!" shouted Woody. Carla stepped forward, about to throw the taper on to *Julie*.

"Stop!" screamed a voice she'd recognize anywhere. "Stop right now."

The flame in her hand blew flat and went out.

Valhalla

Torchlight flickered up the beach, then another beam shone over the sand dunes. Mum was running towards them, calling out and splashing through the water. Carla felt a tug under her arm as Mum grabbed Napoleon's rope. Was this the end of it all? She couldn't believe she had got so far, only to be stopped now. She wanted to scream with frustration. Carla looked at the taper as the ashes separated from the paper and blew out over the water. Mum was gasping as she waded over to them. Her hair blew wildly about her face and she had a torch tucked under her armpit. Carla shrank back. But to her astonishment Mum squeezed her shoulder and took something out of her coat pocket. She fumbled and swore as something plopped into the water.

"Here," said Gus, handing her another taper. Carla watched, unsure what her mother was doing, but at this rate the wind was going to carry Grandpa out to sea despite what anyone did to try to stop it. But Mum wasn't stopping anything. She flicked a lighter, set fire to the taper and threw it into the boat. An instant later there was a *woosh!* and a sheet of blue flame poured over the boat, faster than water.

"Now back," shouted Mum, grabbing Woody by the scruff of his neck. She made him stand behind her. Then she put an arm round Carla and tugged her back, away from *Julie* as the fire took hold, the wind blowing the flames out to sea. Carla watched in alarm as Gus was dragged along and lost his footing. He went up to his neck in water before he stood and let go of the line. *Julie* wobbled and creaked as gold-and-blue flames ran up her mast and flooded her sails with light. Then the wind caught her and she drifted a little way out. Another strong gust and she flew over the waves away from them to deeper water. Then everyone battled against the icy water, pulling on Napoleon's rope to guide them to shore. Carla's cheek rubbed against the rough, damp wool of Mum's coat.

Mum let go of Napoleon's rope only when the water was about their ankles. She tightly grasped the children's hands and they watched as the boat flew away from them. The light from the flames glittered on the water. The fire grew taller, burning away the darkness and flaring up into the sky. Sparks filled the air like fireworks.

"Goodbye, Dad," Mum called.

"Goodbye, Grandpa," called Carla and Woody. Carla

tore her eyes from *Julie* to see a whole line of torches blinking from the sand dunes.

"Goodbye, Grandpa." That was Penny's voice.

"Goodbye, Magnus," called Dad, who must have been standing next to Penny. There must have been twenty or more people now, all gradually coming forward as the boat retreated.

"Oh my goodness, is that Miss Hame?" Carla whispered, watching a dumpy figure wade into the shallows and throw something into the water. Figure after figure flitted in and out of the light, shouting and calling goodbyes and throwing flowers. *Julie* blazed on the water, burning away the darkness.

"Maria had a little boy," Mum whispered. "I delivered him two hours ago. He has no name yet." Carla squeezed her mother's hand, tears pouring down her cheeks. Grandpa was properly out at sea now. The currents were sweeping him way out down the coast in the direction of the Atlantic. She'd done it.

"He's going out fast," said a voice close by. Carla jumped. It was Ern.

"I suppose you had something to do with this," said Carla, eyeing his shadowy face.

"I lied. I'm useless at keeping secrets," said Ern, his teeth flashing white. "And after the carnival tonight, I couldn't even keep this one quiet."

"How did you know it would be all right?" asked Carla, unable to tear her eyes from the burning boat for long.

"I didn't," said Ern. "But everyone knows Magnus would have loved this. Even your mum – especially your mum."

They stood mesmerized by the boat. Fierce fire consumed it as it sailed further and further away until it was just a ball of flame in the open sea. Gradually everyone fell silent. Carla didn't know how long it was before the fire gradually sank into the sea and the light finally went out.

A cheer ran up and down the length of the beach.

"*Well done*," said Grandpa.

"Hey," whispered Carla. "I thought you'd gone out to sea."

"*I'm where I've always been*," said Grandpa. "*I'm in your heart.*"

ACKNOWLEDGEMENTS

Thanks to
John Nash at Watchet Boat Museum
Andrew Carter at Thomas Brothers Ltd
Marion Lloyd for giving me the green light
and everyone who enabled me to write this book!